Built to Win

Lara Rios

Wise Writer Pubishing

Built to Win

Published by WISE WRITER PUBLISHING

Monteil-Doucette, Liliana 1967-

Built to Win Lara Rios - First Edition 2026

ISBN: 978-1-931627-17-7 (Print-Trade)

1. Sports Romance – Fiction

2. Enemies to Lovers Romance – Fiction

3. Contemporary Romance – Fiction

4. Latino Romance

Book Cover by The Killion Group Inc.

Contents

Praise for Lara Rios's Novels

Conquest

Her characters come to life right before your eyes from the very first word.

—Robin Peek - Under the Covers

Lara Rios pens an enjoyable romance with a unique premise in Conquest.

—Rickey R. Mallory - Painted Rock Reviews

Ms. Rios humanizes Tess and Logan by showing their family relationships and the forces that made them the people they are. She shows their strengths and vulnerabilities, their tenderness and passion, and intersperses the serious with the humourous.

—Jane Bowers - Romance Reviews Today

Ms. Rios succeeds in bringing out the best in both characters and leaving the reader wanting more.

—Addicted2Romancebooks.com

Lara Rios has a nice breezy style to her writing and keeps you interested in her charming characters.

—Suzanne Coleburn - The Belles and Beaux of Romance

"A big, beautiful novel of love, family, and the close-knit community they inhabit. By turns touching, funny, tragic, and triumphant, it's the story of an endearing group of people in search of their own American dream."

—Susan Wiggs, New York Times bestselling author

"Julia Amante understands the ties that bind all families regardless of culture and nationality—the struggle for identity, the importance of dream, and above all, love. I truly enjoyed Evenings at the Argentine Club."

—Jill Marie Landis, New York Times bestselling author

Built to Win

Lara Rios delivers a dynamite story rich with emotion, deeply passionate characters, and breath-taking sensuality!

—Best Selling Temptation author, Janelle Denison

Unforgettable characters in a compelling story about the enduring spirit of the heart.

—Meryl Sawyer - author of TRUST NO ONE

CHAPTER ONE

July

Multicolored race cars circled the small track. Fire engine red. Metallic green. Yellows. Blues. Some fast. Some trailing behind. They created a dizzying blur of color in the scorching heat typical of the Bakersfield desert. Occasionally, a car pulled off to the side or onto the middle of the track, and a driver popped out of the window.

Gabriela Alende approached the chain-link fence separating the empty public seating from the racetrack where the drivers practiced for that evening's race. She placed her forehead on the chain-link fence, closing her eyes. She longed to block out the painful memories that resurfaced with every passing car. But even with her eyes closed, the revving engines and acrid smell of gasoline only reminded her of the awkward, lonely years of her adolescence that she had desperately tried to erase from her mind.

She opened her eyes and stared absently at the cars tearing across the track as dust from the surrounding area drifted in the air. Just the sight caused a tightness in her throat, suffocating her. What kind of solace had her father gotten from these loud, dirty tracks? Gabriela drew a deep breath and eased back a wisp of light brown hair that had worked loose from her orderly French braid.

As she turned, her eyes traced a path over the empty stands—bleachers stretched out in neat rows, the metal seats glinting in the harsh desert sunlight. By tonight, families would occupy almost every seat, and perhaps this was the one thing she recalled with fondness. The lively race crowd differed from fans of other sports. Maybe because so many kids attended with their parents and ran around waving flags. The atmosphere was comparable to that of a carnival more than a sporting event.

The fun actually began hours before the race started. Only after buying food and memorabilia of their favorite car and driver at the various vendor trailers would the fans sit and enjoy the race. How many times had she witnessed the same scene? The last time had been three years ago when she and her father had parted ways. She shook her head. In some ways, it felt like just yesterday.

"Track's not open yet." A gruff female voice called. "Can I help you?"

Gabriela squinted past the bright sunlight. She drew a second steadying breath to mentally bring herself back to the present, and she regretted it instantly. The smell of exhaust made her nauseous. "I'm Gabriela Alende. I'm—."

"I know who you are." The tall, athletic woman stopped in front of her. "I'm sorry about your father."

Gabriela nodded. For the last two weeks, she'd had to endure endless phone calls and visits from people who were sorry. She was sick of hearing those words. What exactly were they sorry about? All she wanted was to get past her father's death and move on with her life. "I received the beautiful bouquet from the speedway with all your condolences. Thank you."

"I'm Billie, by the way, the announcer." She held out her hand.

She shook Billie's hand.

"So, what brings you here?" Her eyes strayed to Gabriela's clothes as she released her hand.

Gabriela wore a lavender sundress and two-piece platform sandals with two-inch heels, a fashion better suited for a stroll through a museum. She obviously wasn't dressed for a day at the track. Maybe this was the last way she could rebel against her father. Or perhaps merely a way to deny what she was about to face.

"My dad's car," she said.

"Yep, number 58."

"I'd like to speak with the driver, Cruz Ortega if he's here."

"Should be in the pits getting ready for tonight." Billie looked at the track. "He's not out practicing yet."

"Can I get into the pits on my own?"

"Come on, I'll take you. You're not pulling the car from the circuit, are you?" Billie's slender frame walked gracefully in front of Gabriela, leading her toward the pit area. She wore a black racing jumpsuit with the speedway's red logo emblazoned on the back, and her long hair was pulled into a tight ponytail.

The ground beneath their feet was hard and uneven, the surface littered with crumbs of tire rubber and bits of debris from the track. Gabriela wasn't sure what she was going to do. Of all the crazy things for her father to leave her—a race car. "I need to talk with Mr. Ortega. He probably knows the car better than anyone."

Billie nodded. "You're right there."

She followed Billie behind the track, where some cars were in various states of being repaired while others were parked and ready for tonight's race.

They stopped beside a shiny, royal blue Ford Taurus with the white number 58 painted on the side. The hood was up. Three men with grease on their hands were pulling things out of the engine.

"Don't change the spark plugs until after the first race," said the one bent over the engine.

"Cruz." Billie tapped the man's solid arm.

Cruz looked over his shoulder, keeping one arm in the car. Gabriela got her first glimpse in years of Cruz's rugged heart-stopping good looks. Dark, thick eyebrows cast a shadow over his eyes; sultry, pink lips; short, wind-tossed black hair. He straightened. "Hey, Billie." His eyes flickered over Gabriela, and he frowned. "What's up?"

"You've got a visitor."

He glanced at Gabriela again. "What's she want?" he asked Billie.

Why was he acting as if she weren't standing right behind him? Gabriela stepped closer. "I need to speak with you."

His frown remained, his forehead full of creases, and his eyebrows drawn together. "All right. Speak."

Gabriela looked at the others staring at her. Somehow, she'd pictured being able to discuss her business somewhere different. How could they hold such a personal conversation with engines revving and roaring to life—with so many people around? "It concerns this car."

"I figured it did, Miss Alende."

So, he remembered her. She felt a spark of pleasure for the first time since walking onto the speedway grounds. "The car is my responsibility now that my father's gone."

"Yeah," he said. "Guess I expected he'd be leaving it to you."

She inhaled, trying to read his cold gaze. "Well, I didn't. It's the last thing I expected him to leave me." Especially since he knew how much she hated the track.

Cruz crossed his arms and leaned his backside against the car door. He'd matured and filled out. She noticed how the fabric of his shirt stretched tight around the thick bands that formed his upper arms and how his torso narrowed to sexy, slender hips.

"Beggars can't be choosers," he said after staring at her for several moments. "An American saying, isn't it?"

She wasn't sure what he meant by that, but she didn't like his attitude. "I need to figure out what to do with this car."

"Yes, you do."

"I hoped you might be able to help me."

"How?"

Gabriela swallowed. "I don't know much about racing."

"No." He uncrossed his arms and placed his hands on the car behind him, repositioning his hips slightly, distracting Gabriela. "You didn't exactly hang out at the track when your father was alive."

Oh, yes, she had more than she cared to remember. She'd spent every weekend for twelve years trapped at these speedways while her father neglected her. The moment she turned eighteen, she went away to college to get as far away from her father and the racetrack as she could. Cruz probably didn't remember, and she wasn't here to argue with the driver. Let him believe what he wanted. "Which is why I need your opinion on—."

"My opinion?" He laughed. "How about a fact? This was a game to your father, but it helps pay my bills. Opinions aren't important here," he said.

"I understand."

"So now what? You tell me."

"Well, okay, we keep racing, I suppose. I'll learn whatever I have to to keep the car on the track."

He raised an eyebrow. "You mean you're going to keep running the car?"

"Yes." Was she? She wasn't sure what she wanted to do; how could she sound so decisive? Maybe because he seemed to be challenging her, and she could never resist a challenge.

He smiled. "Great. So, I can still count on a paycheck." He pushed off the car and stood.

"Mr. Ortega—."

"Cruz."

"About paying you . . .." Gabriela shifted on her feet, uncomfortable, unsure how to tell him.

"What about it?"

"Well, it might be a little difficult at first. My father left me this car but nothing else."

Cruz's eyes widened. "Nothing? What do you mean by nothing? Your father's business, properties, and investments are worth millions."

"Nothing. This car is my entire inheritance."

Cruz lifted his chin as if understanding. "He left you a hundred-thousand-dollar car without the means to maintain it." He shook his head. "That's funny."

"I'm glad you think so." She adjusted her purse and straightened her back. "Look, what I'm trying to say is I have no extra money, just the car."

The frown reappeared. "What about maintaining the car, traveling, my salary? How do you intend to pay for those things?"

"I don't know. It can come from what we earn, I suppose."

Cruz glanced at Billie, then behind him at the guys listening with interest. He took Gabriela's arm. "Let's go for a walk."

They left the pits together, walking side by side until he led her beneath the bleacher stands. The moment they stopped and faced each other, the contrast between them was striking. She stood before him in a clean dress with not a wrinkle or stain in sight. Meanwhile, Cruz's T-shirt was torn at the collar, and smudges of grease covered his chest as if he had wiped his hands on the fabric. This morning, she had applied a delicate lavender lotion to her fair arms and legs after her shower. In contrast, his face was darkened by car exhaust and glistening with sweat. He carried the scent of grease and cedar aftershave. But Gabriela suspected that their differences ran much deeper than just appearance or artificial scents.

"A racing team costs money," he said.

"I know—."

"And you don't have any?"

"No, but—."

"Then you'd better forget about racing the car." He lifted a foot and placed it on an iron bar, and leaned his back on a support beam, looking at ease with himself and his surroundings.

"But you'll make money, won't you? In fact, I'm counting on it. If you win a few races, we'll have enough to maintain the car, and I can pay my personal bills."

He shook his head. "Doesn't work that way."

"Why not?"

"Just doesn't. If you aren't prepared to dump lots of money to keep the car running, this is our last race."

Gabriela didn't have a penny, didn't he understand? "Cruz, I'm not going to spend money on this car? I want it to make me money."

"It won't."

She pressed her fingertips to her forehead, where her freshly manicured nails scratched her skin lightly. Her temples began to throb. All those years she spent attending races, and she'd never bothered to learn the business or what her father actually did to run his car.

She assumed that as the owner, her father sat back, watched the races, and cashed a big check at the end of each night. It wouldn't make sense for him to pay for a car that was draining him financially. Not only didn't it make sense, it wasn't in his nature. Carlos Alende never in his life did something that lost him money. Obviously, Cruz didn't know what he was talking about. "If you keep racing and win, you'll make money, right?" she asked.

Cruz laughed. "Oh, I can, and with that, you'd be lucky to buy the guys a beer at the end of the night and refuel the car."

"You're telling me there's no profit?"

He stood upright and came closer to her. "I'm telling you, the expenses are tremendous. I'm also telling you that if you expect that car to win many races, you're out of your mind."

"But why can't it? Aren't you a good driver?"

This time, he frowned. "The point is," his voice turned cold. "The car is old. It constantly needs replacement parts. It's not a winner; it's a racer."

Gabriela sighed heavily. "Replacement parts?"

"Engines, tires, and that's just for starters."

"Well, the car must make more than enough to cover those kinds of expenses."

He rolled his eyes, looking upwards, then swept his hand across his sweat-drenched brow and into his scalp, moistening his coal-black hair. With obvious irritation and fading patience, he faced her anew. "This is the Southwest Series. We don't make money, Miss Alende; it's just fun."

"No, this is a business. I've driven three hours in the desert heat to get here, and all I want to hear is that you'll keep racing the car and win so we can use the prize money to keep us all from starving."

He shook his head. "Have you heard anything I've said in the past ten minutes?"

"You don't understand. I don't have anything else to fall back on. This is it." She swallowed the lump in her throat. The past few weeks were beginning to take their toll on her. Reality was setting in—she was broke. Worse than broke, she had nothing now, no one. She needed just one person on her side.

His eyes narrowed, and he stared hard and cold at her. "Am I supposed to feel sorry for you, Gabriela?"

"No, I–."

"You asked for my opinion. Here it is. Sell the car, take whatever money you get, and run." He gave her body an intimate scanning. "This is positively not your thing, Querida." He turned and walked away, ending their discussion without a care about what would happen to her.

"Cruz, wait." Gabriela reached for his arm, desperate to make him understand. At twenty-four years old, she'd never worked a day in her life, but she was willing to. She'd spent the last six years in college as an art major. She supported herself with a few thousand dollars her father automatically deposited into her bank account every month.

But all that was gone. She had used the money to live on, travel, and buy art, always figuring she was young and had plenty of time to decide on a career and find a job. Now, she wished she had been more responsible. But she never dreamed her father would die so young and give his entire estate away to charity. If this car didn't make money for her, she didn't know how she'd survive.

Cruz looked from her hand on his arm to her face. "What?"

"As long as I own that car, and you're under contact to drive it, you have to do what I tell you."

His eyes hooded, and the color of his face darkened. He turned completely around and faced her, looking like a thundercloud hovering above her. "Gabriela, you're a young woman, a child still. You are not going to hang around a track full of men, and you are definitely not going to tell me what to do. Understand?"

She stiffened, lifting her face to meet his eyes, unwilling to let him intimidate her. Who was he calling a child? "I will be at every race from now on, Cruz. You'd better get used to it."

He moved closer. One arm shot out, and he gripped one of the bleacher's criss-cross supports over her head. She took a step back, but her eyes remained locked on him as she stared at his handsome face.

"You think I don't remember who you are, Gabriela? Because I do."

What did he mean by that?

"You might not remember me," he continued.

"Of course, I remember you." He was a skinny kid when her father hired him seven years ago, not much older than she was. Sweet. He didn't speak much English.

"Do you?" His voice dripped with disdain, challenging her. "You remember when your dad walked out of the office the day he hired me, and that you kissed me? Remember that?"

"No." But she did. She'd sat in his office, off to the corner drawing, pretending she wasn't paying attention. But couldn't keep her eyes off Cruz. He was beautiful and seemed so eager to get hired and to please her father.

Cruz smiled cruelly. "No, huh? Why would you remember? You were just having a little fun with one of your father's lowly drivers. Isn't that right?"

She could only stare into his challenging black eyes. At seventeen, she'd thought Cruz was the sexiest, most masculine man she'd ever seen. Just arrived from Mexico, he was different, exotic, tempting. But it was the innocence in his eyes that had captured her. She didn't see any of that anymore.

He moved closer; his face was just above hers. Their lips almost touched. She saw the film of moisture on his temples and brow, smelled his aftershave, and felt the heat from his body.

"Kiss me again," he said.

She swallowed, gazed at his lips, then at his stony eyes. "Step back," she said.

"Or?"

She narrowed her gaze, wondering what it would feel like to connect her knee with his groin.

Then, all of a sudden, he released his grip on the bleacher above her head but didn't step back. He lowered his head, his lips practically touching hers. "Aren't you going to stop me?" He whispered.

"I'm waiting to see what kind of asshole you've become."

He chuckled, then eased back.

She sighed, relieved. Already, she was envisioning his hard kiss, feeling him parting her mouth with his own sensual, full lips, and inserting his tongue. He left her with the longing for his taste. Damn him.

"I'll tell you again, this is no place for a beautiful, young, pampered girl like you. I'm the closest you're going to find to a gentleman here. Goodbye, Gabriela."

She watched him retreat, too stunned to react. She touched her lips as if he'd actually pressed his to hers. Had she heard him correctly? Had he said she was beautiful? She closed her eyes and tried to clear her mind. What did it matter if he thought she was attractive? The only thing she needed from him was for him to drive the car well, win races, and make money. But he seemed so sincere when he said that wouldn't happen.

She turned and headed to her car. She wasn't angry at Cruz. He made it clear that if she paid him, he'd keep driving. Her normal life had suddenly turned upside down. She was afraid, anxious, desperate . . . not angry. Above all, she was disappointed that the race car would not be the save-all money-maker she had expected it to be. What would she do now?

Cruz returned to the car and reached for his gloves in the toolbox.

"What did she say?" Danny asked.

He slid each hand into a glove and squeezed his fingers open and shut. He shouldn't have gotten so close to her, damn him. "Nothing."

"What do you mean, nothing? Is she still going to race the car?"

Danny was young and energetic and passionate about cars, but he was also a pain in the rear at times. Cruz shrugged and moved past Danny, trying to remember what he'd been doing under the hood.

Danny leaned on the car beside Cruz. "Man, she's hot. I mean, if you can get past that miss hotshot attitude. Did you check out her–?"

Cruz straightened and hit his head on the inside of the hood. "Shit," he yelled. "Don't you have anything to do?"

Danny gave him an innocent look. "You're in a lousy mood."

"I'm racing today, in case you've forgotten, and I'd like the car to run. Do you mind?"

"All right, all right." Danny went around the car to finish his work.

Cruz tried not to think of Gabriela as he labored with the engine but found it impossible. After seeing her again, practically touching her, imagining her soft lips against his, his mind and body wanted nothing more than to remember.

He'd seen Gabriela maybe a dozen times in the past seven years, usually arguing with her old man. As the years went by and she'd changed from an immature seventeen-year-old to a woman in her twenties, he'd often daydreamed about kissing her again. In his imagination, it certainly never happened under a bleacher, with him sweating like a pig.

He'd always pictured her smiling, inviting him to kiss her, then to undress her, begging him to make love to her. He pushed away from the engine and yanked off his gloves.

"What's the problem, Cruz?" Danny wiped his brow and drew a grease stain on his forehead.

Why was he doing this to himself? Gabriela Alende was not the kind of woman he'd ever want. She wasn't nurturing or compassionate. Her interests and tastes were completely different from his. She dressed in clothes he imagined were so expensive, he couldn't afford them even if he spent his entire salary. Besides, he knew she was a cold, heartless bitch.

All she did was sponge money off her dad. A man Cruz would have walked through fire to please. But not Gabriela. The only thing she was close to was his wallet. "I guess that Alende chick got to me more than I thought."

Danny shook his head and laughed. "Heard she can do that. Yep, heard some really wild stories about her and the old man."

Cruz frowned. And they were all true. He still didn't understand why she didn't adore Carlos Alende as much as he had.

"Heard she flirted with the drivers, conned them out of beer, drove the old man crazy," Danny continued. "Did you know her then?"

Cruz shook his head and thought about the kiss she'd given him years ago. She'd done more than flirt, but he wasn't about to tell Danny and add to the gossip.

"I've got a headache," Cruz moaned. The back of his head was throbbing. "I'm going to get something cold to drink, okay?"

"Hey, relax, Cruz. I'll finish this, and Flip will be back soon. He went to buy us some burgers."

Cruz nodded. As he strolled away, he lit a cigarette. He blew out a puff from the side of his mouth, relaxing. Between his late-night racing schedule, janitorial work, and morning college classes, he was physically drained. He couldn't wait for the race season to be over so he could rest. He'd be out of the extra pay, but at least he'd catch up on his sleep. Of course, with Gabriela Alende being the new owner, he would probably be out of a racing job soon, anyway.

He missed Carlos Alende already. The pep talks he would give him, the pats on the shoulder . . . a man who understood hard work and loyalty, a man Cruz had admired like no other. That was precisely why Cruz would never be able to comprehend the distance between Gabriela and Carlos Alende. Didn't the woman realize what a treasure her father had been? Didn't family mean anything to her?

Cruz was close to his parents. He never would have disrespected them the way she did, Mr. Alende. In Mexico, Cruz helped his father at the auto shop every night. After going to school all day, he would put in another five or six hours working on cars so that his father wouldn't have to hire a helper. He'd missed out on some of his childhood and teenage years, but he didn't mind because he was making life easier for his father. He would go out of his way to please both his parents.

Gabriela and Mr. Alende didn't have that kind of relationship. Even at his funeral, she stood with no emotion on her face during the service. Immediately afterward, she walked away without listening to or acknowledging anyone's condolences.

What kind of woman didn't cry at her father's funeral?

He reached the concession stand, which was not yet open, but the girls always let him buy something before the race. He peeked inside the booth. "Hey, beautiful. Sure could use a large coke."

The cute eighteen-year old bent over, getting paper cups from a plastic bag, lifted her head, and smiled. "One soda coming right up." She filled a large cup, placed a lid on it, and handed it to him.

He gave her five dollars and winked. "Gabbyas. Keep the change."

She didn't speak Spanish but seemed to like to practice with him. "Muy gusto."

Cruz laughed. "Mucho gusto. Although, what I think you mean is de nada."

She shrugged sheepishly. Her mother walked in then. She and her three daughters ran the booth. "Still trying to pick up on my daughter, Cruz?"

He smiled. "Naw, just buying a Coke. Your girls are too smart to get involved with a guy like me."

She smiled and hustled around the grill, setting frozen hamburger patties at equal distance from each other. "If they were a little older, or I was a little younger, we'd snatch you up in a heartbeat, and you know it."

Cruz laughed and turned away. He was starting to feel better. He didn't know why he let someone like Gabriela Alende get under his skin. Just because the car now belonged to her didn't mean his life had to change. His driving record was pretty good. If things didn't work out with her, he could find another team to drive for and keep that badly needed extra income.

Of course, keeping the woman out of his thoughts would not be so easy. He'd been fantasizing about her for so many years that it would be difficult to stop. The Gabriela of his dreams was gentle and loving. The impression of the sweet seventeen-year-old still stayed with him, and he found that, for some reason, he had always wished their paths would cross again. Now that they had, and he was faced with reality, he wished Gabriela had stayed in his fantasy world.

CHAPTER TWO

August

Gabriela watched as two men carried away all her possessions. She had lived in this home for six years, but like everything else, it belonged to her father, and he'd left it and his other five properties to a cancer research charity. Cancer had taken her mother from them when she was six years old and changed both their lives forever, so she couldn't be bitter about his decision. But without a home, she had no use for furniture, and she needed cash, so she agreed to sell everything to an auction house.

"That subhuman ass," Sheena said, crossing her arms and shaking her head as they watched the room become vacant.

Gabriela forced a smile as she looked at her best friend. With her thin body and long legs, Sheena looked better than any model in Vogue magazine, but her mouth was better suited for a truck driver. "Are you referring to my father again?"

"How could he do this to you?"

Gabriela shrugged. She didn't care about the money, but she wished her father had at least left her a small amount of cash to live on until she could figure out how to support herself. All he'd willed her was that broken-down race car she had no idea what to do with. "He put me through college and supported me for six years. He didn't owe me anything more."

"He was your *father*. And he disinherited you for no reason."

It hurt that he hadn't thought about what would happen to her, his only child. But then again, he hadn't cared about her when he was alive. Why would he be any different in death? "And I wasn't that great a daughter."

Their last fight echoed in her ears. Insulting accusations and ultimatums on his part, defiance and disrespect on hers. He was too traditional. He disapproved of her friends, roommates, and lifestyle and accused her of being immoral and out of control. But he didn't know her. She'd gone through a rebellious stage, sure, mostly to capture his attention, but it didn't last long. Alcohol, drugs, and random sex weren't ever her scene as he assumed they were. She'd always felt what he really disapproved of was that while she was at college, she was no longer under his direct control.

Because she'd been hurt, and because she wanted to hurt him back, she'd confessed to all the horrible things he accused her of doing, when in reality, she spent most of her time in her apartment that she'd converted into an art studio or traveling to museums in foreign countries. He'd threatened to disinherit her then, but Gabriela hadn't cared. In a fit of tears and pain stemming from years of living with an unloving father, Gabriela wished out loud that her mother had been the one to live, not him.

As the cruel words slipped past her lips, she'd instantly regretted the outburst, but the sad truth was that she'd meant it--unlike Carlos Alende, her mother would have loved her. The only thing he loved was his business. Either way, those were the last words she'd ever said to him three years ago.

He'd quietly agreed that it would have been best for all of them if God had taken him rather than his wife. Then he told Gabriela to leave and never come back.

Sheena shook her arm. "Did you hear me?"

"No, I'm sorry. What did you say?"

"I said, parents are supposed to love their kids unconditionally. All teenagers behave crazy, but your parents aren't supposed to give up on you."

Tears clouded her vision. "I have a throbbing headache and feel kind of dizzy. Can you get me a glass of water, please?"

"Sure." Sheena kissed her cheek and left the room.

Gabriela pushed open her French doors, letting the jasmine-perfumed breeze fan her face. Behind rows of Italian Cypress, the sun made its descent. She drew a deep, steadying breath. The time was right for her to move. She'd finished college and needed to get on with her adult life. She'd wasted enough years studying things like classical sculpture.

But entering the business world and leaving the protective arms of her college town was frightening. Although interesting to her, she doubted many employers would be impressed with her ability to recognize figures carved into the balustrade around the Temple of Athena Nike.

"Miss, can you sign here?" A voice called behind her.

"Just a minute." She wiped her eyes.

"Miss, we have to get going."

She turned around. Her living room was empty. Without reading anything on the form, she signed it. The thin young man handed her a check.

She took it and glanced at the amount that would help her survive for two or three months if she was careful. "Thank you."

He nodded and turned around.

"Hey, Gabby, that guy is taking stuff from your bedroom. Didn't you say you didn't want them to go in there?"

Coming out of her lethargy, Gabriela noticed the art easel box the blond, larger guy had in his hand. Panic clutched at her heart. "Hey, wait, not that box. I told you guys, nothing out of that second bedroom."

"It just has trinkets and junk. But the box itself is cool."

"I'll take it." She took the box out of his hands.

He shrugged. "Whatever." He left without another word.

"I'll check and make sure they didn't take anything else," Sheena said, her light Auburn hair drifting behind her.

Gabriela kneeled with her box in the middle of the empty living room. Junk. It might be junk to him, but to her, they were priceless things that belonged to her mother. A little wooden cross she hung over the doorway to keep their home and all who entered safe under God's protective spirit. A scratched and dented silver jewelry box passed down from three generations of grandmothers. A Virgen de Guadalupe statue which her mother kissed every morning and every night . . .. All things her mother had kept even after her father had begun making tons of money and had been able to buy her expensive, high-quality artifacts. Yet, her mother still preferred her own simple belongings.

Gabriela wiped away tears that had reappeared and rolled down her face. This was getting her nowhere. She needed to load this box and her suitcases in her car and drive to Sheena's place.

"Everything's in there," Sheena said as she strolled back.

"Thanks for letting me stay at your place until the end of the month. The dump I rented should be ready by then."

Sheena crouched beside her and took the box out of Gabriela's hand. "Like you really have to thank me."

A white envelope slipped out of the box and sailed to the floor.

Gabriela picked it up and stood, staring at her name written across the front.

"What's that?" Sheena asked, balancing the box on her hip as she stood beside Gabriela.

"Letter from my dad. The lawyer gave it to me."

"What does it say?"

Gabriela glanced at her friend. "Don't know. I didn't open it."

Sheena stepped closer. "Why not?"

"The last thing I need is one more of his moralistic lectures."

Having listened to Gabriela's end of phone conversations with her father more than once, Sheena's face softened. "That's true, but you can't leave it stuffed in this box unread forever. Read it."

Gabriela ran her finger along the sealed seam. Her father's last words—in a sealed paper envelope. How appropriate. Just as he'd kept his love for her, guarded, released only on rare occasions. She placed the envelope back in the box. "Someday."

Sheena gave Gabriela a quick hug. "Are you ready to go?"

She nodded. "I'll get my bags and meet you downstairs."

Once she had filled the trunk with her suitcases and her back seat with her computer, cameras, easels, and art supplies, she drove away without even one backward glance at her home of six years.

"What the hell do you mean you're docking me a whole hour's pay?" Cruz tried hard to control his temper.

"Hey, you come in late, that's what happens, Cruz." The fat, lazy janitorial supervisor reluctantly lowered an iPad that he used to play games and lifted a Styrofoam cup full of black coffee.

"Late?"

"Last week, you clocked in ten minutes late, remember?"

Cruz hated how he talked to him as if he were too stupid to understand. "Ten minutes? I can make up ten minutes."

His supervisor shook his doughy face. "You have to learn to follow the rules, Cruz. They're there for a reason."

Cruz tightened his hold on the broom, lifted it, and turned around. "Yeah, to screw guys out of their money."

"What did you say?"

He knew he had to watch his mouth. There were plenty of guys who'd take his job if he were fired. He'd been reminded of that enough times. One Mexican was as good as another. "I'll get here on time from now on," he said.

"You do that, Cruz."

Cruz left the small, cramped office and flung the broom down the hall. One more year, he kept repeating it as if it were a mantra. One more year, and I'll never have to clean toilets, sweep and mop floors, or take orders from an idiot like that again.

Upon graduation, Sheena moved back in with her parents as she planned her wedding to her college sweetheart, Griffin. She'd been planning the wedding for two years, and though her parents weren't pushing Sheena to move out, they adored Griffin, and they increasingly dropped hints like, "Honey, we'd like to take a winter cruise, but we don't want to do it if you plan to have the wedding soon." Or, more pointedly, "Let's create your wedding registry this weekend. What do you say?"

Sheena evaded the topic each time her mother mentioned it. Gabriela asked her one night when they went to Williams Sonoma to shop for a wedding gift for one of their friends why she wasn't making more progress on her own wedding plans.

Sheena shrugged. "We're not in any hurry."

Handing Sheena a lovely glass bowl with swirls of green and blue colors to match the bride's home color scheme. "He's not in a hurry, or you're not? Because you seem really hesitant to give your parents a date."

Sheena took the bowl and put it back. "*We* are not in a hurry."

"I know he's preoccupied with finishing his education." Griffin was getting his Ph.D in Film and Media Studies, and he was always either writing or producing documentaries or was "on location" shooting something. Maybe Sheena was feeling ignored, or that she wasn't his priority.

"He is, but being married wouldn't affect his finishing his degree. It's not that. I could plan the wedding tomorrow if I wanted to. I just don't."

Gabriela nodded and dropped it because Sheena was getting defensive about it.

Sheena handed her an air fryer. "This is more practical," she said.

"Do we want to give her a practical gift?"

"Yes, marriage is practical." Though Sheena wasn't eager to get married, she did spend most of her time with Griffin. So, while Gabriela stayed at her place, she hung out with her parents or sat in her room alone, trying to decide what she could do to make money.

Tired of being inside, Gabriela drove to downtown Santa Barbara. As she passed the small cafes, quirky boutiques, and tiny art galleries that gave this part of town its charm, she envisioned opening up her own art store, but that took money.

She stopped at one gallery and impulsively asked to speak with the owner.

"He's not here, but I'm the manager. Can I help you? Was there a piece you were interested in?"

"Actually, I'm an artist, and I was hoping to bring you some of my pieces. Maybe he'd be interested in showcasing them?" Galleries weren't likely to take a chance on an unknown like her, but it was worth a try.

The manager offered a tight smile. "You're welcome to drop off your portfolio. Include your artist statement, your contact information, website, and places your work has been displayed, and we can determine if you'd be a good fit for the gallery."

Gabriela nodded and took their card. "Thank you."

She strolled to the nearest cozy cafe, ordered a latte, and sank into a leather chair to sip the steaming drink while considering what she'd just learned. The only places her work had been displayed were at the university. And a website? She thought back to her classes; only one of them focused on marketing and sales. Creating a website and adding a virtual gallery of her work wouldn't be too difficult, but she had to be practical. She needed money now. Her passion was art. She loved capturing the world through her paintings and intricate sketches, and her professors told her she had talent. But could she really make a living by following her passion?

She swirled her drink and looked up at the barista. Maybe she could get a job making coffee for a while as she worked on placing her pieces in various galleries. Maybe.

As she gazed out of the window at the cars cruising by, thoughts of the race car returned, angered that the thing was worthless. If her father was going to leave her a car, why not one she could actually drive? Instead, he'd left her a problem.

Cruz had effectively chased her away. She hadn't been back to the track. For all she knew, the car was no longer racing. Since she hadn't paid him, maybe Cruz had left it abandoned, collecting dust in some forgotten corner of the speedway yard. Part of her was okay if it sat there and rotted, relieved that she didn't have to deal with the stress and pressure of learning about the business of racing and managing a racing team. But she couldn't ignore it too much longer; she'd have to decide what to do with the car soon.

Standing and dropping her empty coffee cup in the trash, she returned to Sheena's place. She'd invited friends over for a dinner party and drinks. Her heart wasn't in socializing of any type, but it was better than moping and worrying about her future.

CHAPTER THREE

September

Gabriela tossed the feather duster into the trash. "Yuk. You'd think they would have done a better job cleaning up this place. Especially after making me wait so long to move in."

Sheena wrinkled her nose at Gabriela's newly rented apartment. "Come back home with me. *Please*."

"I can't live with you and your parents forever. You all have been more than generous, but I can't stay with you any longer." Gabriela plopped onto the ugly rented taupe couch she'd picked up at a thrift shop. She could have sworn dust released at impact. She coughed. "Don't worry. This is temporary."

Sheena shivered. "I hope so. Call me if you change your mind. My parents don't mind, trust me; they love having you around." She moved to the front door. "I have to get going. Griffin's parents are taking us out to lunch. He's been working on a documentary on the life of a gamer who sold tech secrets to the Chinese, and his parents know someone in the FBI or DHS who has inside info on this. He's super excited."

"Wow, sounds fascinating."

Sheena nodded. "I know. He geeks out about all this. I'm going because he promised we'd go to Skylight Books after lunch for an author event and book signing. And I'm going to hold him to it. Love you," she said and slipped out.

Gabriela glanced around her new home after the door closed, and Sheena was gone. She swallowed the lump in her throat. This little rat hole could never be a home, but she was good at making things look beautiful. She'd hang some of her art and visit estate sales to find a few inexpensive chairs and other furniture. She'd make it livable.

With a sigh, she dragged her suitcases full of clothes into her bedroom. She unzipped them and began storing her undergarments and casual tops in the drawers she and Sheena had wiped clean earlier and left to air out.

The closets were small, barely large enough for all her dresses and skirts. She noticed paint peeling on the inside and only one bar, which was splintering, to hang her clothes. It probably wouldn't hold much, so she'd have to replace it. She hung only a few items and left the rest in suitcases.

After finishing in the bedroom, she went into the tiny kitchen and opened the empty cupboards—more filth. She groaned. She hadn't had time to go grocery shopping yet, but she needed to add more disinfecting spray to the list. Taking a water bottle from her refrigerator, sat at her kitchen table to rest for a moment. Sipping from the bottle, she stared at all the boxes strewn around the living room. Tonight, she'd tackle that tonight, but now she was too tired to continue.

When she finished her water, she lifted the box with her mother's mementos from the small rectangular coffee table. She pulled out her father's letter. "*So you had to have the last words, huh Dad?*"

Gabriela rested her back against a wall and sighed. Things could have been so different between them—should have been different. She should have been at his side at the end, holding his hand, not reduced to reading lifeless words on a sheet of paper. She slid her fingernail lightly along the seam, debating whether to open the envelope. What could he possibly say to her in a letter that would make any difference now?

She tore at a corner of the envelope, slowly inserted a fingernail into the tear, and opened it along the seam. She might as well get it over with. If not, the letter would haunt her every day—every time she saw it in the box. She slid down the wall and, with shaky fingers, unfolded a handwritten letter from her father, written three years ago—after their final fight.

Gabriela,

As I write this letter, I realize I have failed miserably as a father. I can think of a million things I should have done better. Perhaps my biggest mistake was to keep you with me when your mother died. Your grandmother in Mexico wanted you, but I promised your mother I'd keep you. As you know, I had no idea what to do with a little girl. And I certainly don't know what to do with a defiant teenager.

I tried to love you, but I didn't know how. You've always been a stranger that I couldn't relate to, and I'm sorry. Perhaps I was never cut out to be a father. Perhaps without your mother, I didn't want to be. I wish things could have been different.

If you're reading this letter, it's because I've passed on. While alive, I've lavished you with money and things, and all it's done is produce a spoiled, self-indulgent young woman.

My will has been read, and by now, you know I've left you my race car. Auto racing was the only thing I remember you enjoyed as a young girl. When your mother was alive, and we went as a family, you loved it. When you got older, you didn't seem to care for it anymore, but I have a feeling it was to spite me. Anyhow, you can sell the car for at least twenty thousand dollars or continue to race it. If you choose to invest the time to learn, you might be able to make some money with it.

However, knowing you, you'll go for the easy cash. Contact Terrell Morrison at the Irwindale Speedway. He'll buy the car.

I hope you understand what I've done. Money never made either of us happy. Start over, Gabriela. Go visit your family in Mexico. Above all, have a good life.

Your Father,

Carlos

Gabriela balled up the letter and stretched her arms out across her knees. She bent her head and closed her eyes, and renewed pain swept over her. Not even in his last words could he tell her he loved her. This was nothing new, so why did it hurt so much?

Tears stung her eyes, then flowed down her face as if a pipe had burst inside. She allowed them to come full force this time, sobbing loudly for endless minutes, letting all the pain pour out, her throat becoming sore, her shoulders shaking, her lungs inside aching. She threw his letter across the room, and it rolled under the couch, out of sight. "You bastard," she cried. "You cold-hearted bastard."

She wiped her face and stared at the ugly, unfamiliar room. He was right about one thing: she would start over. And if this was the place where she had to start, then so be it. Running both index fingers under each eye, she caught the remaining tears. She'd paint and refinish the kitchen cupboards and install a closet organizer, whatever it took to make this place bearable, and as for work . . ..

She stood impulsively and found the box the lawyer had given her, containing information on the race car and the driver. Carrying the box to the small, olive-green kitchen table, she spent the next couple of hours studying financial statements, the driver's win history, and the car's performance. Grabbing her laptop, she searched the internet to try to understand what those numbers meant.

Could she really race the car? She covered her face with her hands, massaging her forehead and temples. She thought about her father's words, how she'd take the easy way out. As she leaned back in her chair and stared at the paperwork, her thoughts circled around one true fact. Carlos Alende never taught her to be anything but dependent on him, then criticized her for needing support.

Gabriela pushed herself out of the chair. Well, no more. As of today, she would depend on no one. As ridiculous as it sounded, as impossible as it might be, she'd take the race car and make it a winner. She'd show her father. And herself—because if she was honest, she'd never believed much in herself either.

She took her car keys and left her apartment. Outside, she looked up at the sky, wondering if there was a heaven and if angels above watched over the lonely souls stuck on earth. She'd wondered that often when her mother died. *Are you watching me, Dad? I'll race that car, and I'll make money on my own. Even if you never thought so, I'm tough enough to do it. In fact, I was always strong, even stronger than you.*

Gabriela sat in the stands beside Flip, the team's crew chief, while the drivers practiced. She liked Flip, a no-nonsense man, about her father's age—probably late fifties.

Cruz took the car around the curves masterfully. He drove with skill and confidence. Although she didn't know much about racing, she did realize he wasn't an amateur. He might be racing in amateur circles, but the way he controlled the car told her he was a professional. "He's good, isn't he?"

Flip narrowed an eye, half looking at her and half watching the car. "Cruz? Yeah, the boy's got talent."

"So, if he's a good driver, why aren't we making any money? Cruz told me my father was actually taking a loss. I checked through his records, and it's true. Owning and running the car cost my father thousands of dollars."

Flip nodded. "I don't think your father was in it for the money."

"No, I'm thinking it was probably a tax write-off."

Flip shrugged. "Could be. Don't know much about that kind of stuff."

"But why didn't he make money? I thought the sport paid well."

Flip shook his head. "Not at this level. This is small potatoes."

"So how does it work, Flip? How do we move from small to big races?"

Flip smiled. "You get Coca-Cola, Ford, or Dupont to sponsor you."

She shook her head. "No, come on, Flip. Not everyone has huge sponsors."

He shrugged. "And not everyone makes it to the Winston Cup either."

She was getting more discouraged with each passing minute. She needed money to make money, but she didn't have a cent. Maybe she could apply for a loan or find local sponsors. She had to figure out something. "Suppose I were to find the money? Could we move to the next level and make a real profit?"

"There's three months left of this season. Cruz has more than enough NASCAR points to get him into the Westerns next year, but—."

"What are the Westerns?

"The next division. After the South Westerns comes the Westerns, Bush Series, then the Nationals."

"You know what I need, Flip? Someone to teach me about the business? Will you do it?"

"Well, yes, but Cruz—."

"You leave Cruz and the money to me?"

Flip shrugged again. "You're the boss."

Yes, Gabriela thought, I am, and if anyone is going to organize this team and make money, it will have to be me. Somehow, she'd convince all these men to listen to her, but she had to start with Cruz. She had a feeling that if she convinced him, the rest would follow.

Cruz noticed Gabriela sitting beside Flip when he pulled in to refuel. Flip called out to him and told him he needed to turn tighter on turn four because he was coming close to brushing the wall. Cruz nodded.

Gabriela made no attempt to communicate with him, but she wore a large, white, floppy hat, so you couldn't help but notice her. She sat beside Flip in tan shorts, exposing her long, tempting legs.

When he returned to the track, he forced himself to concentrate on the car, but the rest of his practice session was ruined—he knew she was out there. With each lap, he listened to the sounds of the engine, made sure the wheels were balanced, and tried to tune out the rest of the world.

Inevitably, his mind wandered back to Gabriela. What did she think she was doing? Was she still under the illusion that she was going to travel the circuit with him and the team and continue to live the lifestyle she was accustomed to? If that's what she believed, she was in a dream world. Actually, she just had no idea how racing truly worked, and he wasn't going to be the one to instruct her.

Frustrated by his lack of concentration, he swerved to the left and drove into the pits. He clambered out of the car and went inside to change. When he came out of the changing room, duffle bag in hand, he saw her standing by the car, waiting, her white hat gone. He stopped in front of her. "You're back."

"Did you expect to scare me away with that little stunt under the stands?"

He shrugged. "Was worth a try."

"I don't run away from challenges."

He laughed. "Is that what I am?"

"Don't flatter yourself. I was talking about the car and racing."

"Well, good luck." He moved around her, but she sidestepped and stood in front of him again. He had to hand it to her; she was spirited. "If you're looking for trouble, you're going to find it, Gabriela."

"Actually, my life has turned into one enormous challenge, Cruz."

He sighed. "And?"

"I need your cooperation."

"I'm your driver. I'm doing my job. What else do you want from me?"

"I want to learn about my inheritance." She pointed to the car beside him.

He sighed again, but this time, it came out more like a growl. "Gabriela, if you want to hang out here and learn, it's fine with me. Who am I to stop you?"

"But will you leave if I can't pay you regularly at first?"

"I won't work for free."

"I don't expect you to." She tucked wind-tossed hair behind her ear. "At least not forever, just until I get on my feet."

The mention of her feet reminded him of those legs. He couldn't help but glance at them. Smooth, a perfect toasted honey color, firm, long. He inhaled sharply and forced himself to concentrate on their discussion. "Which will be...?"

"I don't know."

He shook his head. "If payday comes and I don't get paid, I walk. I'll move on to another team with an owner who knows what he's doing and who's going to pay me." Even though leaving her father's team would hurt. He'd been driving number 58 from the start of his career. He now had almost a superstitious connection to that number. This was *his* car, *his* team.

She inched closer. "But I can't make money without a driver."

"That's your problem."

The disappointment on her face slapped him with a strong dose of guilt for being so cold, but he owed her nothing. Why stay? He gave her the best intimidating look he could manage. "Now, if you'll excuse me."

She didn't budge. "I have a plan to keep that car rolling and to make us all a lot of money."

"I don't care."

"Why not?"

"First, because I'm tired, and I want to take a nap before tonight's race. And second, because all I want to hear is that I'll continue to get my paycheck as usual. How you do it is your business."

"That's just it; I want it to be your business, too. I want to pull out of these local races. Enter us in real money makers–."

"Count me out."

She frowned and looked frustrated. "But why? I don't understand you."

He was hot and tired, and although standing next to Gabriela wasn't exactly torture, her expensive-smelling perfume was driving him crazy. "Because I don't give a damn about racing. I do it to make extra cash on the side. I don't want to travel from state to state and live this life full time."

"If that's not what you want, then what *do* you want?"

He shrugged. "When I finish college, I'll be an accountant."

Gabriela arched an eyebrow. "That's what you want to do the rest of your life?"

"Something wrong with that? I've been fixing cars my whole life. Yes, I want a clean, respectable job."

"Of course you do, I just never pictured you . . . it's an admirable goal, Cruz. But . . .."

"But?" He placed his duffle bag on the car roof and leaned against it, resigned. He just couldn't walk away from Gabriela.

"But it will take you years to establish a clientele and build a profitable business even after you get your degree. What if you could earn money fast by entering bigger races?"

He began to shake his head, but she continued.

"Just long enough for you to have a reserve in your bank account, so you don't have to drive part-time anymore or whatever else it is you do to get through college."

He watched the wheels turn inside her head. He'd given up dreaming of making the easy buck long ago, but he was curious. "What do you have in mind?"

"I think I can raise enough money to finance another season of racing, but not here."

"Where?"

"Flip said you have enough NASCAR points to qualify for the Westerns."

Cruz felt as if someone had taken jumper cables to his heart. The Westerns? He stood straight, no longer relaxing against the car. "Do you realize the costs involved?"

"I'll get us the sponsors."

"From where? You have no experience—."

"I'll get them."

"Why, Gabriela? Why are you bothering?" He held out his arms in question. Aside from not wanting her hanging around the track, he couldn't figure out why a woman like her would *want* to be involved in this business.

"Basically, because I have no other options. This car and you are all I have."

"Me?" He tried to ignore the tight feeling in his chest. But those large, light brown eyes, that sweet voice were impossible to ignore. As was the knowledge that someone, especially Gabriela, needed him.

In Mexico, he had a large family, lots of friends, and he would never turn his back on one of them if they needed him. But here in America, he'd changed, hardened. It was every man for himself in this land. He didn't know when he'd become such an unfeeling bastard. Maybe it was a gradual change. However, it happened, he didn't like himself anymore, didn't like the man Gabriela needed so badly.

She stared at him. Awaiting his verdict. Finally, she spoke again. "Please, Cruz. Give it, and me, a try."

He nodded stiffly, not willing to let her see the emotions dueling inside him. He pulled his duffle bag off the car and began walking toward the parking lot. "So, what are you asking me to do exactly?"

She followed. "Help me."

"How?"

"Keep racing, without pay until—."

"No."

"Until," she continued. "I straighten our accounts and find some sponsors."

He could help her get her accounts straight in one week, but he wouldn't offer. They reached his '69 Ford Mustang. He tossed his bag in the back seat and turned to her. "Then what?"

"Then I use the money to fix the car, finish out the season, and get us ready to enter the new division."

He shook his head. "You're asking me to take a big gamble."

"I'm giving you a chance to use your talent and possibly make a lot of money."

"Yeah, which means I have to quit my regular job, my college courses, everything, and make racing my life." Although the opportunity to quit the custodial job appealed to him more than he dared admit.

She stepped closer. "Only for a little while."

"At least a year of full-time racing and lots of traveling. Maybe more than a year if we don't make money right away."

"A year will be enough, and at the end of that year, you could be a wealthy man."

He frowned as he thought about her offer. Interesting. Assuming, of course, she could gather the money to even give them a fighting chance at the Western regionals. "What about now? Your dad has been paying me fifteen percent of each race as well as my salary."

"All right, Cruz, how about this? No Salary, but I'll give you fifty percent once we enter the Westerns."

Every muscle in his body tightened. Had he heard this crazy woman correctly? "Fifty? Five-oh?"

"That's right. Of our net profit, of course, after all our expenses."

He shook his head. He couldn't take advantage of her this way. She'd be taking all the risks, raising all the money; he couldn't share equally in the profits. "That's not the way it's done—."

"I don't care how it's done. That's my offer. Take it or leave it."

He placed a hand on her shoulder and angled his head to look into her bright eyes. "We could make hundreds of thousands at the Western Regionals. Millions with the right sponsors."

She smiled. "That's what I'm counting on."

CHAPTER FOUR

October

Saturday night, Gabriela arrived at Irwindale Speedway early. She sat in the stands and watched Cruz run his practice laps, then drive off into the garage, then after a while reappear and run more laps. She sighed. Her life had never been full of excitement, but could this sport get more boring? Standing, she took her clipboard where she planned to take notes but remained blank except for a doodle she made of Cruz and the car and made her way to the back.

She waited until Cruz drove the car into the garage, got out, and removed his helmet. "Hi," she said.

He glanced at her with a frown. "The owner rarely comes into the garage area."

"Why not?"

He cursed and walked away from her. "Danny, it still doesn't sound right. Let's check out the pistons."

Cruz lifted the hood, then bent over the engine.

Gabriela didn't like being ignored. If she was going to be involved in owning a racing team, she wanted to know all about it.

"What are you doing?" she asked, looking at the engine.

Cruz angled his head, then pushed away from the car. "Working," he said as he squatted and dug through the bottom drawer of the red toolbox.

"What's wrong with the car?"

"I don't know. If you'll leave us alone, then maybe we can figure it out." He stood, tool in hand.

The silver instrument looked much like a weapon in the hands of a madman. She took a step back and pointed at Danny. "Is he the mechanic?"

"You can't afford a mechanic, Gabriela. We have volunteers."

"Well, no wonder the car doesn't run well. We have a volunteer and a driver trying to fix it."

"Dios mio." He shook his head and walked away. He braced his arms on the car and stared at the engine again.

"Why are you discounting what I'm saying? Don't I have a point?"

He ignored her and began fiddling with engine parts.

"We need to hire a proper crew. Where's Flip?"

"Vegas," Danny said."

"Vegas? He's the crew chief; he should be here."

Both men burst into laughter. Cruz wiped his hands on a clean rag and turned to her. "And who told you he was the crew chief?"

"He did."

Danny shook his head. "I'll say this for him; he knows more than all of us put together, and he's almost always at the track. Unless, of course, he gets an urge to gamble. But he's not a crew chief."

"Especially since we don't have a crew," added Cruz. He tossed the rag to Danny and gripped the hood.

She placed her hands on her hips. "Let me guess; he's also a volunteer."

The hood slammed shut, and Cruz turned to her. "You're starting to get the picture."

Yes, she was. They had an old car, a smart-ass driver, no crew, no money. No wonder they didn't win races or make any money. "I want to meet with you after the race, Cruz."

He gave Danny a lopsided grin. "Now that's the best offer she's made me yet," he said to him. Then he slid his bent index finger under her chin. "I'll be waiting for you here in the garage."

Gabriela shifted her face away and frowned. "Good."

Back in the stands, she waited for the race to begin with a bottle of water and books on auto racing. The past few weeks, she'd been researching NASCAR, concentrating on the Westerns. She still had a lot to learn, but what she really needed was a commitment from Cruz. He told her he'd think about it. She'd given him time, but she had to know. If they were going to build this team, she had to start lining up sponsors soon. She opened her books and read about flag colors: green, yellow with a red stripe, blue, red, black, and checkered. They each had expected compliances from the drivers. The meaning of the flags she remembered from childhood; other rules she did not.

Hours later, she glanced up, surprised to find the stands full of people. The overhead lights glowed brightly, cars entered the track, and the first race of the night was about to begin. She had been so wrapped up in the books she hadn't noticed the time passing. Focusing on the cars, she searched for number 58 but didn't see it on the track yet.

She closed her books to concentrate on the race. Maybe she'd understand what was going on. Halfway through the night, Flip showed up and sat beside her.

"You're here."

"Can't win a damn thing in Vegas," he grumbled, shaking his head in disgust.

"Have you been down to the pits?"

"Na. This race is almost over, so Cruz should be out soon." He glanced towards the track with a hint of anticipation. He obviously cared about Cruz and how he performed.

"I'd like to go over a few things with you and Cruz after the race if you'd like to get some coffee or something."

"I could go for a burger."

"A burger." She smiled. "Okay." Flip was so much more cooperative than Cruz.

🏁

At the end of the night, Cruz came in second.

As they walked to the pits together, she asked Flip, "Is the car in good condition?"

"Not really."

"Do you think Cruz would do better with a different car?"

"Oh yeah. He's a good driver."

"Is he? I checked his track record. Only a few wins."

"If you're wondering whether to keep the pain in the ass, I'd say he's worth it."

She silently questioned his worth when they reached the garage, and Cruz's characteristic frown was on his face.

"What happened? Did you lose all your money?" Cruz asked Flip.

"Yep."

Cruz turned his attention to Gabriela. "You lucked out. You found a chaperone."

"I'd like to speak with you both."

Cruz lowered the door to the garage and then walked to the parking lot without another word to either of them or waiting for them to join him.

Gabriela was growing weary of his attitude. She had enough to deal with right now without adding a moody driver to the list. What was his problem anyway?

She and Flip followed him to his Mustang. He tossed his duffle bag in the back seat.

"We can take mine," she said, figuring he'd driven enough for one night.

Cruz shot a glance at her Mercedes Coupe, then glared at her. "What's the matter? This car not good enough for you?"

"That's not what I meant, Cruz."

"Oh really?" He snorted and turned away.

She grabbed for his arm but caught a handful of his shirt instead. She tugged hard enough to make him stop and look at her. "I'm getting sick of your scowl and foul temper."

He yanked his arm loose and took her wrist. "Well then, go home where you belong, Querida."

"And stop calling me that."

He walked her backward and pressed her against his car. "What should I call you then?"

"Cruz, let her go."

"Shut up, Flip," Cruz growled.

"It's all right," Gabriela said. "He's already tried bullying me." She faced him directly. "I'm not frightened."

Cruz smiled, let go of her wrist, and swept the back of his fingers across her cheek. "No, you're not. Maybe you like this kind of rough stuff. Maybe that's why you keep coming back."

She caught his hand, which was tenderly touching her face, irritated at herself for noticing how erotic his rough fingers felt on her skin. "I came back because that car you *lost* with tonight is mine."

Cruz's smile disappeared. He angled his head and looked back to where Flip stood a couple of inches away, looking like he was ready to pull Cruz off her at any second. "Go on to her car, Flip. We'll be right there."

"Hell no," he said.

"Go on, mano. The lady can take care of herself."

With Cruz's hard body pressed against hers, she wasn't so sure, but she nodded. "I'm fine, Flip."

Flip frowned. "Just let her go, and let's get the hell out of here. It's late and cold. You're acting like a damn fool."

Cruz continued to stare at him. Finally, Flip cursed and walked away, mumbling something about youth and testosterone.

Cruz turned to her then. He buried a hand in her hair. "Very brave of you."

"Stop it. Let me go and say what you want to say."

"What makes you think I want to say anything? Maybe Flip is right. Maybe I just want to have my way with you."

She shook her head, unable to bear the feel of his fingers touching her so intimately when his expression revealed nothing but contempt. "I don't see desire in your eyes, just anger and cruelty."

He blinked, lowered his gaze, then stepped away.

Although relieved, she also experienced a faint void, as if some essential part of her soul had been taken away. She crossed her arms, rubbing her cold skin, bothered by the strange sensation.

He swallowed. "Okay. I do have a question. It's about your offer the other day."

"What about it?"

"I've thought it over."

She took a deep breath. "And?"

"Have you told Flip or anyone else about it?"

"No, but--."

"Good, don't."

"What does that mean? Are you turning me down? Or will you work with me and try to enter the Westerns?"

He stepped in close again. His thighs almost touched hers. "Let's get things straight. I don't like you, and I don't care if you ever make money from racing."

The harshness of his voice made her flinch. His strong, masculine body so close made her tremble. "I--."

"I don't intend to be your friend. And remember, you own the car, not me."

She shoved his chest because he seemed to be getting closer and closer, and she couldn't breathe. "Fine, as long as you understand, I could fire your ass anytime I please. So don't push your luck. And stay out of my personal space."

He stared at her, mute. She thought she detected a brief nod. "I'll finish out this season without pay. You make sure that car runs properly."

"Making sure the car is properly maintained is precisely what I want to talk to you about. Now, shall we go? Flip is waiting."

He stepped away from her, raked fingers through his hair, and began walking to her car.

"Cruz."

"What?" he called over his shoulder.

"Why. . . ? What did I do to make you hate me?"

He stopped, but didn't face her. "I don't hate anyone."

"What did I do?" she repeated.

He bowed his head, and she saw how tense his neck and back muscles were. He nodded. "A couple of years ago, at your father's fiftieth birthday party, I handed him a glass of champagne and asked him if he was enjoying himself." Cruz turned and faced her with pure disgust in his eyes. "You know what he told me? He said he'd give everything he had to have you at his party and to have you love him."

Gabriela opened her mouth to say something, but nothing came out. She'd told her father she loved him plenty of times. *He* was the one who never said those words to her. Why would her father outright lie, and why to Cruz?

"You tell me, what should I feel for an opportunistic woman who took advantage of her own flesh and blood? If I had been your old man, I wouldn't have left you a penny either. You're a spoiled, selfish brat and deserve to learn what it's like to work for a living. I have no respect for you, Gabriela. I'll work with you out of loyalty to your dad, but stay away from me, understand?"

Cruz turned away from her again, and Gabriela stood rooted in the same spot, too shocked to move. Cruz didn't know what he was talking about. He never really knew her father if he thought that cold-hearted old man was a loving father, and Cruz certainly didn't know her.

How could she explain that when she lost her mother, she also lost her father? He'd shut her out? Cruz didn't realize that all of Gabriela's troubled adolescent years were just a plea for her father's attention. Cruz was never at any of *her* birthdays where her father 'stopped in' between business appointments.

No, she hadn't attended his fiftieth birthday party. In the past few years, she tried not to see him at all. She'd given up on being loved by him, and took the only thing he offered--money. She sighed, knowing her actions had been wrong. It didn't matter that Cruz had no respect for her. She didn't respect herself, and that was ten times worse.

Flip sank his teeth into his hamburger. Cruz wasn't sure if the smell of French fries came from Flip's plate or if the smell of grease had permeated the walls of the dingy diner. Both Gabriela and Cruz ordered a cup of coffee, and they watched as Flip enjoyed his meal.

Cruz held the cup up to his mouth, took a sip of the bitter, hot liquid, and glanced at Gabriela through the steam. She had been quiet, not meeting his eyes. Guilt for what he'd said to her made him drop his gaze, but he had spoken the truth. She should be ashamed of how she treated her father. Carlos Alende was a good man who had worked hard his whole life. He was honest. And he'd given Cruz a chance to make money in this country when no one else would.

He put down his coffee cup and stared at the black liquid. His vision blurred as tears moistened his eyes. Cruz still couldn't believe Mr. Alende was gone. But he was. He'd watched it happen right before his eyes. One second they were talking, and the next, Alende was lying on the ground, clutching his chest and gasping for breath.

Life had a funny way of changing when you least expected it. Mr. Alende never went into the pits. Why that day? Cruz blinked to clear his eyes. He looked at Gabriela. Mr. Alende's last words to him were, 'Tell Gabriela that I loved her.' How could he tell her something like that, and would she even care?

Cruz sighed. "Well, you got us here, *boss*. What do you want?" His voice sounded tired even to himself.

She gave him a harsh look. "I want a list of the people we'll need to build our team. I already figured out we need a real mechanic." She leaned closer to Flip. "You're the unofficial crew chief; how about we make it a paying job?"

Flip stopped mid-bite. "What do you mean?"

"I mean, we need to organize a team. I want you to be in charge of it."

Flip shifted his vision to Cruz.

Cruz nodded. "Yeah, you heard her right. She thinks she's going to enter us into the Winston West next season."

Flip placed his burger back on his plate. "No kidding?"

"I have to raise the money," she said, caution in her voice.

"And you think you can?"

"I do."

Flip smiled and looked from Cruz to Gabriela. "And you two are going to work together?" His gaze remained on Cruz. "And act civilized."

Cruz sighed, then nodded. Flip knew him and that he'd never hurt Gabriela or any woman, but he'd behaved poorly tonight, and both he and Flip knew it. "I'm in," he agreed.

"Oh yeah." He took each of their hands and squeezed. "This is better than Vegas."

Cruz looked at Gabriela; a mixture of fear and excitement gleamed in her eyes, and he wondered if he should dare to hope.

CHAPTER FIVE

November

Gabriela crossed off another potential sponsor. The past couple of months had become endless days and nights of watching races, going to practices, hiring crew members, getting loans, and calling businesses trying to find sponsors. So far, all she'd gotten were lots of maybes once Cruz qualified for the Westerns, entered, and proved himself. They'd keep an eye on number 58. That was all good, but didn't get her the startup money she needed to purchase a hauling trailer and touring coach, or to pay the bills that kept piling up on her kitchen table.

She tossed the clipboard onto the small desk she'd squeezed between the wall and her bed in the small one-bedroom apartment.

"Damn," she said out loud as she paced. What was she going to do? They needed sponsors.

Her phone rang, so she picked up the cell, hoping, praying that one of the business owners was returning her call.

"Gabriela? Where have you been? My parents said you haven't called or visited."

Gabriela recognized Sheena's voice. She sat on the bed. "Trying to stay alive."

"I hear you're going to race that car your dad left you."

"That's right."

"When did you decide this?"

"I left you a message two months ago. Where have you been?"

"After going to D.C. with Griffin for two weeks, where he interviewed this guy for hours every day, he told me he needed to fly to fricken Romania to do more interviews, so I went to Mexico to visit mi Abuelita. She's getting old, you know?"

"And you had this sudden desire to see her?

"I didn't want to fly back home. Once I was there, I realized I should stay a few weeks. I took a lot of pictures, wrote some music, and talked to her every night after her amazing dinners. Anyway, it was therapeutic."Sheena had a Scottish mother and Mexican father and was deeply tied to her roots and family. Gabriela envied her. "I never got to know my grandmother. I talked to her on the phone a few times when I was little. My mom talked about her family all the time, but my dad rarely did."

"I think your dad was an outlaw who ran north to start a new life. Maybe that was why he was such an asshole."

Gabriela laughed. "He was too boring to have such an exciting past."

"So, tell me about this car."

She sighed and leaned on the headboard. "I'll probably have to sell it and find a job in a fast-food restaurant before the month is out."

"Why? Can't you make a fortune with one of those cars?"

"That's what I thought. I'm learning it takes a fortune to run it."

"Well, get rid of it, and let's open up the art school we always talked about. I'll be the director of dance and music, and you'll do the art and sculpture, remember?"

Gabriela laughed. "And where are we going to get the money to do that?"

"I've got about fifty thousand in a trust fund."

"That's supposed to be for your wedding and to start your life with Griffin. Plus, we can't even get a year's lease on a building with that." She absently played with a ring on her right hand, spinning it around her little finger.

"But it's a start."

"No, it's not. I need money now. I can't wait two or three years for something like that to take off. Besides, we'll need about half a mil to really open and run an art school."

Sheena groaned. "How much can you make with your race car?"

"I've been studying this a lot. Some teams make millions, depending on the sponsors they get and what division they run. The first thing to do is to ensure that my driver qualifies for the Westerns. Then I *need* to find some sponsors, or it's all over."

"Getting investors shouldn't be hard. Come on, Gabriela, with all the rich people your dad knew."

Gabriela had already thought of contacting the people her dad did business with, but she wanted to race this car on her own. She didn't want people giving her money because she was Carlos Alende's daughter. She had to succeed on her own merits. "I can't go to any of them."

"Why not?"

Sheena wouldn't understand, but Gabriela tried to explain regardless. "It would be too much like asking my father for money. I don't want his help."

Sheena made an unladylike snort. "He's dead. He can't help you. What are you talking about?"

She shook her head and slid off the bed. "When this is over, I want to know I failed or succeeded on my own."

Sheena sighed. "You're living in a dumpy apartment, using rented and second-hand furniture. I didn't see anyone knocking on your door, offering to help you. You are on your own, in case it hasn't hit you yet. Give yourself a break, will you?"

"Yeah," she said silently. "It's hit me, all right."

"Then do what you can to raise money and get that car doing whatever it does to make big bucks. You're a businesswoman now, Gabby."

Sheena was right. Business was business. She'd be offering these companies the opportunity to invest advertisement dollars in their team. A chance to be part of NASCAR. "I bet my dad's partner, Rob, would help sponsor the car."

"There you go, now you're talking. Why don't you hold a benefit dinner, invite all the deep-pocket people, and hit them all up?"

Gabriela began to pace in front of the bed. If anyone would help her, it would be her father's partner. Although he had witnessed many of her shouting matches she'd had with her father, Rob never seemed to judge her—at least, he was always kind. "A benefit dinner," she said, beginning to like the idea. "Yes, that would work, but where would I hold the dinner? I don't have money to rent a place."

But just as she spoke the words, she knew she could persuade Rob to not only sponsor the car but allow her to use his house for the benefit dinner. She had no choice; she had to contact people who could afford to invest in her car. She stopped pacing. "Listen, Sheena, I'll call you back."

As she stepped into her father's old office, the familiar, lingering scent of pipe tobacco hung in the air like a ghostly presence. An odd shiver ran down her back as if the room itself held onto memories of him. To be back in 'his territory' and not see him behind his desk was unsettling. After all, this was his home more than their actual residence.

Rob stood behind his desk. "Gabriela, come in. How are you?"

She stared at her father's shelves, which used to be full of family pictures, mostly of her mother.

"I've boxed up all your father's things, Gabby, waiting for you to claim them, but no one could find you."

She faced him. "My mom's pictures . . .."

"In the boxes."

She nodded, swallowed the lump in her throat, and tried to compose herself. This was no time for a display of personal emotions. "Rob, I'm here on business."

"I'm really sorry about how things worked out. If you want to come work for the company—."

"No," she nearly laughed. The last thing she wanted was to work for her father's company. If he hadn't spent every waking moment working, they might have been able to develop a relationship. She hated this company. "I do have a request, though."

"Anything."

She smiled. "My dad left me his race car."

Rob's cheeks turned a deep shade of pink, contrasting against his pale complexion, and his body shifted slightly as if uncomfortable. Perhaps he didn't agree with her father's final decisions regarding his estate. "I heard."

"The car's a disaster—falling apart, but it's finished the season. I'm trying to raise money to enter the team into NASCAR's Winston Western Series. We don't have sponsors, and we desperately need some." She was surprised at how strong her voice sounded when her stomach was in knots.

"You'd like me to sponsor the car?"

"I'd like my dad's company to sponsor the car. It seems only right."

"Of course," he said immediately, almost eagerly.

"I'd also like a list of the people he did business with so I could invite them to a benefit dinner and try to get more sponsors."

"Sure, I'll have your dad's secretary get that for you."

"One more thing."

Rob waited.

"Can we hold the benefit dinner at your house? I don't have a home anymore."

Rob leaned forward and took her hand. "Gabby, are you okay?"

"I'm fine."

"Half of this company should be yours. I feel terrible."

"Don't." Gabriela squeezed his fingers. "Dad left you the business because he knew you'd know what to do with it. I wouldn't have wanted it."

"You shouldn't be scrambling to make a living."

"Maybe it's precisely what I need to be doing."

Rob lifted her fingers and kissed them. "You've grown into a beautiful young lady." He smiled. "And, of course, you can use my home."

That evening, she strolled into the pits with her clipboard. Her relationship with Cruz had not improved in the past two months. All he did was scowl at her all the time. According to him, her ideas were always way off base. They had shouting matches in the pits, which always earned either him or her a cheer from the guys. But he kept racing, and she kept learning about the business, and trying to increase the funds in their bank account.

As she approached him, he left the car's side and began walking out of the pits.

"Hey," she called after him. "I need to speak with you."

"I'm going to wash my hands."

"Wonderful," she said sarcastically. "I'll wait."

A few minutes later, he returned. "What now?"

She took a deep, controlling breath. Sometimes, she wanted to slap him; she really did. She knew expecting him to respect her as his employer was asking too much, but at least he could be polite. "We're going to a benefit dinner next Friday night, so I need you and Flip to show up dressed in suits."

Cruz gave her a blank stare. "What's a benefit dinner?"

"It's our last hope of getting the money we need. If this doesn't work, we can go back under the bleachers, and you can give me a kiss goodbye this time."

He grinned for the first time in months.

She turned away from him, but he reached for her arm. "Gabriela?"

She noticed the guys had all stopped working and were watching as if their daily comedy show had begun.

She gave Cruz a questioning look.

He moved in close as if to whisper. The intimacy of his breath on her ear sent a disquietingly pleasurable sensation to the pit of her stomach.

"I've got a suit, but I doubt Flip does," he said.

His deep, quiet voice made her gaze into his dark eyes, which, for once, looked serious and warm. "Come to the announcer's booth before the race. My purse is up there. I'll give you my credit card. Take him and buy him one."

Cruz nodded.

"Cruz, buy yourself one too; it's a business expense. I want you both to look perfect."

Cruz grinned. "Si, *senorita*. My new life goal is all about being perfect enough for you."

With an arched eyebrow, which told him she'd believe that when hell froze over, she walked away.

Cruz felt a hand on his shoulder. "Well, I don't see steam coming out of your ears, so I guess she didn't piss you off this time?"

Cruz shifted his gaze from Gabriela's perfectly shaped backside to Flip's dirty mug. "She's set up a benefit dinner and wants us both dressed up."

"Us?"

"You and me, old man."

Flip smiled, obviously pleased with all the confidence and control Gabriela had bestowed upon him. "That girl is just like Carlos."

Cruz frowned. "In what way?" Gabriela was nothing like her father.

"When Carlos came to this country, he was dirt poor. We worked together doing odd jobs." He shook his head; his eyes had a distant look. "I took that nice, secure city job; he built his own company. Had the same look in his eyes Gabriela does, same drive, same determined set of his chin."

Cruz shrugged and wiped his jaw on his shoulder. "Yeah, whatever you say." He walked to the cooler and pulled out his water bottle. Tipping his head back, he guzzled half the liquid in the small bottle, enjoying the iced water going down his throat.

Flip stood in front of him again. "Give her a chance, boy."

"I thought I was."

"Are you?"

"Flip, come on. She's asked us all to quit our jobs and follow her on this crazy venture. Why? Because she needs money. Shit, I should have my head examined for doing this to begin with."

"No one's twisting your arm. You can do what I did and take the secure job. I made that mistake once by not listening to Carlos when he asked me to go into business with him. His daughter is giving me a second chance, and I'm taking it."

Flip went back to the car. Cruz sighed. Did he really want to examine why he was doing this for Gabriela? He tossed the water bottle back into the cooler. Hell.

CHAPTER SIX

When they arrived in the picturesque suburbs of the Palisades the evening of the benefit dinner, Rob greeted Cruz and Flip with a firm and enthusiastic handshake. He then turned to Gabriela, offering her a warm kiss before gently wrapping his arm around her waist, guiding her into the house.

As they stepped inside, the familiar elegance of Rob's home welcomed them. Tasteful furnishings, reflecting his wife's sophisticated style, filled the living and dining rooms. Tonight, however, there was an added layer of charm: the tables were adorned with crisp, vibrant tablecloths and colorful floral arrangements, all thoughtfully in the team colors, creating a festive and inviting atmosphere.

Rob generously agreed to cater the benefit dinner and pick up the tab.

Gabriela wanted to wrap her arms all the way around him—show her gratitude for his support. After working with Carlos Alende day in and day out, Rob knew every detail of the turbulent relationship she'd shared with her dad. He'd even witnessed some of their arguments. Yet, he was still willing to help.

Gabriela looked around the familiar house where she'd spent so much of her childhood after her mother died. Rob's wife, Jolie, had become the default babysitter every time her father would forget to pick her up from school or was just plain too busy to care for her. The house had always been lovely, and although Jolie had added some nice new artwork and done a bit of redecorating, the home essentially remained the same.

"I've got three servers to handle the guests, plenty of food, and lots of champagne. We're all set."

Gabriela rested her head on his shoulder. "I hope this works tonight, Rob."

He patted her back and kissed the top of her head. "It will, Gabby."

"Where's Jolie?"

"Had to work, but she told me to tell you to call. She's upset that she hasn't seen you since the funeral. She wants to see you and do whatever it is you ladies do when you get together."

Gabriela nodded. "I will, I promise."

People began arriving. Rob and Gabriela greeted them. She introduced Cruz to each new guest. Although he stood beside her, shaking hands politely, he appeared uneasy. His unsmiling and tense expression spoke volumes. He set his jaw tight, and a tiny muscle twitched on his muscular, sexy neck. He rolled his shoulders every few seconds and seemed to struggle with standing still. She wondered if the formal setting was making him uncomfortable. Of course, with Cruz, it was difficult to tell. He seldom looked happy around her.

Later, while everyone, including Flip, stood about the room drinking cocktails and eating appetizers, Cruz stood off to the side alone, his coat open, one hand in his pocket, looking at the backyard through a sliding glass door.

Not used to seeing him in a suit, she took a few moments to admire his trim, beautifully built body: his erect posture, solid frame, broad chest and shoulders. In her experience, it was a rare man who could look wonderful in both everyday clothes and formal wear. *I bet he looks terrific in nothing at all.* She smiled. She was allowed an appealing thought every once in a while, no matter how inappropriate. Purposely, she approached him.

"The view is amazing, isn't it?"

He turned his head and ran his gaze down her body. "Nice dress."

She smiled even though for some reason—maybe the edge in his voice, she didn't think it was a compliment. "Thank you."

"This is your scene, isn't it, Gabriela? Fancy houses, food with exotic names, champagne?"

She eyed him quizzically. Something else about her he didn't like? She just couldn't win. "Rob was my father's business partner. Did you know that?"

Cruz nodded.

"Yes," she said.

"Yes, what?"

"Yes, I grew up in places just like this."

Cruz watched her, his face displaying no emotion. "You must miss it."

She shrugged. "Some things, yes. But not the things you might think."

He angled his head; placed both hands in his trousers' pockets. "What do you miss?"

She gazed into Cruz's eyes. Was this a challenge, or did he really want to know? *Prove you don't miss the money, rich girl.*

She took a breath and looked around Rob's living room. "My father took everything with him. The house I grew up in, the furnishings . . . I can never walk into a room in my house again and remember, picture Thanksgivings with my mother, see the kitchen where she made me breakfast, sit in my old bedroom where I slept and hung out with friends, laughed and cried. It's like that entire part of my life never existed. He erased it all." She returned her gaze to Cruz. There. The truth—whether he believed it or not. "That's what I miss."

Cruz frowned, but his eyes seemed to soften. He lifted a hand out of his left pocket, and she thought he was going to reach for her, but he slipped it back in. He nodded.

Did that mean he understood? Cruz was a tough man. "Want to walk around with me a bit?" She asked.

"Is that what I'm expected to do?"

She hooked her arm in his. "Yes, pretend you're enjoying yourself."

Cruz walked beside her, trying to ignore how terrific she smelled, and not think about the way the silky blue material of her dress molded to her back and bottom.

He'd always thought she was a beautiful woman, but lately, at the track, he'd begun to think of her as cute. She marched around with her baseball cap and jogging gear, clipboard in hand, trying to act tough. And the way she stood up to him and gave him hell—it was difficult not to smile or outright laugh along with the guys. But tonight . . . she was way past cute. She was ravishing and elegant and . . . he wasn't sure he wanted to start seeing her like that again.

She chatted with everyone, full of charm, enticing them with her wide, honest smile and stunning eyes that seemed to caress you when they landed on you. People couldn't help but be drawn to her. They seemed to sincerely like her. If he wasn't mistaken, admiration gleamed in their eyes as they looked at Gabriela. Even he was beginning to take to her, despite all he knew.

What he'd seen at the track these past few months was nothing like the spoiled girl Carlos Alende had described. And what she'd just revealed about losing her family home opened up a whole new side of Gabriela. He couldn't help but feel for her. How would he feel if he could never return to his parent's home where he'd grown up, where his soccer trophies still sat on a shelf in his old room? Where everything was still as he left it.

After having to socialize way too long and being displayed like a circus animal in front of a bunch of rich people, they were seated and treated to a fancy dinner.

During dessert, Gabriela took his hand and squeezed it. "Okay, wish me luck."

As quickly as she'd touched him, she let his hand go, and Cruz wondered if she knew that the slightest contact with her sent his nerve endings into high alert. She didn't. She was nervous. He could see it in her eyes. "Time to dance, huh?"

She nodded.

He wiped his mouth with a white linen napkin and sat back in his chair, wishing he could do something to help. But this was her stage, not his. "Give it your best shot."

Gabriela stood and went to Rob's side to make her announcement. She smiled and stated everything simply. She was running a race car in honor of her father. His company name would be on the car since Rob was the major sponsor, but she was looking for others.

All signs of nervousness seemed to have evaporated from her demeanor.

The room grew silent for a few seconds, and Cruz glanced at Flip. Gabriela was crazy to think these rich people would want to lay down good money to run their car. Feeling sorry for her, he wanted to rescue her from the disappointment which was sure to come.

But then, after many congratulations, they started shooting questions at her about the races, his stats, her plan, the chances of qualifying and winning. She fielded their questions like a pro, and it even looked like some people were getting excited. Cruz straightened in his chair, leaned forward toward the dining table, and watched what was happening with closer attention.

Gabriela announced his driving percentages and her marketing plan, which sounded outlandish to him and made his future seem so grandiose;

Cruz wondered if she was still talking about their team. She sold them a dream. Be part of the fastest-growing sport in America. A family sport. A clean sport. A sport where athletes still shake hands with and value their fans.

Then, the most bizarre thing happened—she began to get offers. Full sponsorships and some partials. Names of other companies that might also help were suggested. Gabriela collected so many business cards she had to empty part of her purse to make room.

Cruz was in awe. Rich people were amazing. They were willingly throwing money at her—at them. Just to have their company name printed on a race car. He couldn't believe it. He stared from her to Flip. *Well, I'll be damned*. It looked like Gabriela was really going to do it. She would raise the money to get them into the Winston West.

At the end of the evening, Cruz and Flip walked Gabriela to her car. The luminous smile on her face made her irresistibly attractive. Cruz fingered the keys in his trouser pocket as he watched her with growing interest. For the first time, he was pausing to really look at her, not just on the surface, but inside the real woman. Tonight, he'd also listened. He found he liked what he saw and heard. Gabriela was much more than a beautiful face and a great body. She had a gift he lacked—Gabriela was a brilliant speaker, a saleswoman.

He didn't want to let her leave just yet. For some reason, he felt a connection to her, and he wanted to explore it further. "How about a celebration drink?"

"You and Flip go. I'm exhausted."

He wished Flip had brought his own broken-down car tonight.

"I'm worn out too, Cruz," Flip groaned. "You two kids go. I'll drive your car home, Cruz."

Cruz glanced at Gabriela. "I'm game. Where's your car?"

"Right here, but—."

"The Kia?" Where was her Mercedes Coupe?

She nodded.

Cruz tossed his keys to Flip and, before she had a chance to stop him, slid inside her car.

"Get in. Let's go," he said when she opened the driver-side door and looked in at him.

Reluctantly, she got into her car. "Cruz, really, I'm tired."

"Just a cup of coffee then. Come on."

She started the car and watched him warily. "Then what do I do with you?"

"Drive me home." All he wanted was just another hour with her.

"Mmm," she said, not seeming to like that idea in the slightest. "All right. Where to?"

He gave her directions to a quiet bar close to his home. She nodded and drove silently.

He stared intently at her profile, a mixture of curiosity and confusion swirling in his mind as he pondered the enigmatic nature of her cold and hot personality. During their arguments, she'd get right in his face and confront him with unwavering intensity, her eyes blazing and her voice unfaltering as she stood her ground without hesitation. Yet now, sitting side by side, she appeared uncharacteristically reserved, her demeanor subdued and her gaze focused on the road. Of course, this was the first time they were truly alone, just the two of them, enclosed in the intimate confines of the car.

"Mind if I put on some music?" Maybe that would relax her.

She glanced at him and shrugged. "Go ahead."

He played with the scanner a bit until he found a Spanish station. A soft romantic ballad drifted through the compact car, stirring parts of his body and making his heart beat faster. He watched her for a reaction and received none. He sighed. Maybe extending the evening had been a bad idea. They had nothing in common.

At the bar, they found a corner table, and he ordered a beer, while she ordered coffee.

"You were amazing tonight." He stretched out his legs and crossed them at the ankles. "You did good, Gabriela."

"*We* did marvelous. It will take weeks of meeting with these people to set up the paperwork, but since this season's over, I have the time."

He smiled, feeling warm and lazy. "I guess I won't get that goodbye kiss after all."

She smiled into her coffee mug. "Not yet."

Giving in to his need to touch her, he reached across and covered one of her hands, which she had wrapped around her mug. "We don't have to wait until the end to share a kiss, you know?"

Her eyes flashed, and she stared at him. "What are you doing?"

He caressed the back of her hand with his thumb. "What do you mean?"

"I mean, we've never spoken two civilized words to each other, so what's with the sultry music in the car, this bar thing, this hand-holding? Enlighten me."

He shrugged, stopped caressing her hand, but continued to touch her. "Just being friendly."

"No, you're not."

He stared at her, wondering what she meant. He *was* trying to be nice to her. "You and I are like two cars." He moved his hand back and forth above hers. "When we get too close, bam, there's sparks." He covered her hand again. "I was just wondering if we could make them positive sparks rather than negative all the time."

"Oh really? Well, stop wondering, the answer is no."

"Why not?"

"You asked me once if I remembered that kiss when we first met," she said.

He nodded.

"I thought you were so gorgeous. I loved your voice, your accent, your kind smile. In your eyes, I saw passion, promise, and maybe even innocence. I thought Dad had finally hired someone with character. Every time I looked at you, I melted inside. I may have been an impulsive teenager, but I loved that kiss."

He grinned, suddenly excited about the prospect of getting closer to Gabriela. "Me too. I—"

"But after seven years in this country, you've become a cold, angry jerk with a chip on your shoulder a mile wide."

Cruz pulled his hand off her and sat back. "Well, don't hold back. Tell me how you really feel." He reached for his beer and took a drink.

"What happened to that guy I kissed seven years ago?"

He slammed his mug on the table. "What do you think? Do you know what it's like moving to a country where you're always ridiculed for the way you speak, look, and the work you do?"

"Oh, and what a perfect excuse to feel sorry for yourself and act like an ass."

Anger heated the blood rushing through his veins. He no longer cared what she wore or how good she smelled. Once she opened her mouth, all he wanted to do was stuff a sock in it. "I do not feel sorry for myself," he said between clenched teeth.

"You walk around angry at the world, and everyone—."

"If you had to work as hard as I do just to survive, you might not treat the world as if you owned it, either."

She leaned across the table. "Just what the hell do you think I'm doing? I hit the pillow at night, and I'm asleep before I can turn out my night lamp. I'm working just as hard as you are."

"Well, you've been doing it for a few months. Let's see how happy and positive you are in seven years."

She straightened. "You've done well for yourself, Cruz. You've put yourself through college and supported yourself in a foreign country. You have a lot to be proud of. Too bad you can only see what you haven't got." She lifted her purse and hooked it over her shoulder. "Can we go now?"

His neck and jaw muscles were so tight he thought they'd snap. "You go. I'm within walking distance of my place."

"Are you sure? I don't mind–."

"I said, go."

"Fine," she stood and walked around the table.

Cruz watched the sway of her hips molded by that hot dress as she walked away from him. Gabriela was a real beauty and way beyond his reach. Had he really thought he could connect with her? Women like Gabriela weren't interested in working men like him. Sure, maybe temporarily, she'd get a thrill from being with him, but eventually, she'd want to return to her own crowd.

He took a long drink and watched her step out the door. Besides, even if she were interested, he didn't know how to talk to her. He wiped his mouth and growled. But he wanted to, damn him. He cursed and ran after her. "Gabriela."

Almost at her car, she stopped and looked back.

"I want to make sure you get safely inside your car."

She didn't argue. They walked silently around the back end of the Kia. He opened the door for her. "Where's your Mercedes?"

"Sold it." She stepped behind her car door but didn't sit.

"What? Why?"

"It's the only thing I owned outright. I needed the money to live." She gripped and tugged softly at his suit lapel. "I have bills to pay."

He looked at her sexy fingers with clear, white tips. Yeah, like the suit he wore tonight. "I'll pay you back for these clothes, Gabriela, I—."

She shook her head, no longer looking angry. "I'm not asking you to."

Unable to resist, he reached across and touched her shoulder, running two fingers up along the side of her neck, tracing a vein that hid behind her ear, wanting to feel her pulse. Her soft skin was like lotion on his fingertips. He quickly glanced at her eyes for a sign of disapproval and saw none, then focused on her delicate neck again.

She'd sold her car . . . to build their team. She was giving everything she had, all the while he accused her of being a spoiled rich girl. He wanted to apologize. He wanted to hold her. But could he? She didn't appear to want to get closer to him. Or had she said she'd consider it if he changed his attitude? All he knew was that she'd enjoyed his kiss seven years ago. "You're right, you know?"

She swallowed and eased her head to the side, away from his touch. "About what?"

His hand slipped down from her neck, along her shoulder to her lower back. He pressed gently and took a step closer. "Sometimes all I see is what I haven't got, but that's a good thing because it keeps me striving for more. Does that make sense?"

She braced her hand on his shoulder as if to keep him at a distance, but her gaze roamed his face. She had a soft expression in her eyes. Then she shook her head. "It's not a good thing. Open your eyes, Cruz. You're a fighter and a winner. I've always seen that."

To Cruz, it was as if someone had gripped his heart and was slowly squeezing. This was the Gabriela he'd always dreamed of—soft, adorable, and approachable. He cleared his throat. "Thank you for . . . seeing me that way."

"You're welcome," she said like a caress.

"Can I admit something to you?"

"Maybe."

"When you kissed me as a teenager, I was scared shitless and I was tongue-tied. Even though you were amazingly sexy, and I was instantly turned on, you were the boss's daughter," he said. "Also, I didn't know if you were teasing me or if you really liked me."

"I really liked you." Her eyes were locked with his.

In his youthful insecurity, he'd assumed she'd been playing with him when she'd actually been attracted to him. He'd blown it. But maybe it wasn't too late. He could tell she still felt this tug between them. He saw it in her eyes, in the way she allowed him to stand so close to her, how she let him caress her back. His fingers fanned the expanse of her ribs.

"It's a nice memory we'll keep tucked away, okay?" She ran her hand down his arm and eased his hand away from her body.

"I am still attracted to you, Gabriela."

"Don't, Cruz. Don't say anymore."

With his index finger, he tipped her chin up. "Okay, I won't."

"Don't kiss me either."

He smiled. "I wouldn't dream of it." But that's all he wanted to do. He maintained eye contact with her, wishing she'd be the one to stretch on her tiptoes and kiss his lips. Place her hands on his body—somewhere, anywhere, as long as she touched him.

"Good night," she whispered.

With reluctance, he stepped away from her. "One of these days, Gabriela, I'll be holding you, and it won't be outside or beside a car, and you won't ask me to let you go."

He thought he detected regret in her eyes. "We're not those young kids on the racetrack anymore, Cruz. We're adults with responsibilities, and . . . well, we're on our way to something big. I feel it now, don't you?"

"That means nothing to me; you know that."

Her eyes sparkled. "It means everything. Freedom. Our future. You and I are going to make this happen. Together. But we have to stay focused on what matters."

He dropped his hands in his pockets again. What was she talking about? All he knew was that she was as attracted to him as he was to her; he'd felt it, so why not pursue it and see what happened? He wasn't that timid kid from the racetrack anymore; she had that right. He wouldn't be brushed off so easily this time. "Drive safely."

She climbed into the car, closed the door, and glanced at him through the window. Then, with one last soft smile, she drove away, and the distance between them grew.

"How did it go last night?" Sheena asked as she handed Gabriela a steaming cup of strong espresso that reminded her of her favorite little café in the Latin Quarter in Paris. Those were good days when she spent a year studying and practicing art abroad—days were long gone.

Gabriela folded her legs and sank into the pillowy sofa covered with pastel flowers, sipping her coffee. This bright home that felt as if they'd captured a bit of spring and kept it trapped forever inside, was so much nicer than her depressing apartment. Sheena didn't realize how lucky she was to live here. "How did it go?" Gabriela echoed.

Sheena, of course, meant the benefit dinner, but all Gabriela could think of was Cruz. "Unbelievable." Like shockwaves, the heat kept coming back. Cruz stood so close, his body touching hers. Creating inner yearnings she wasn't sure she recognized or wanted to feel, but had nonetheless kept her up all night, wondering. Somehow, she'd had the strength to set boundaries. Like she'd told him, they had to stay focused on their goal. Building the team. Winning future races. Making money.

"Are we getting closer to our art school?"

"We're getting closer to the ARCA-Menards series. Are you ready to get to work?"

Sheena twisted her lips, giving her a sour look. "Me? What do you want *me* to do?"

Gabriela pulled out a file folder stuffed with sponsorship forms, business cards, and notes. "If you're not doing anything, I could use your help. I have about twenty-five possible sponsors. Half of them wrote checks last night; the other half said they'd consider it but didn't commit to a sponsorship level. I need to contact them all and get them to commit as much money as possible and draw up contracts. I have tons of work to do. Will you help me get started?"

Sheena sighed and took the file. "As long as you don't expect me to join your team, Gabby. I can't think of anything more distasteful than hanging out at a racetrack."

"You'd be hanging out in my apartment. At least until I get us a permanent garage with an office."

"Screw that. I'm not working in your apartment. Let's get the garage and office first." Sheena said.

"Well, we can do that. Rob's check will cover the lease of a building for the season."

Sheena looked in the file folder. "Holy shit, Gabriela! Look at how much money these people gave you."

Rob would be the primary sponsor at $250,000. Her father's business logo would go on the roof of the car. But no one else would come even close to that. This was Rob's way of possibly giving her what he thought she deserved as Carlos Alende's daughter. "Don't get too excited. Every time an engine blows on one of these stupid race cars, it costs thirty to fifty thousand dollars to replace. I'm figuring it will run me around $50,000 to pay for the crew. Then there will be travel expenses and entry fees for each race, which can run up to $10,000. Can you believe that?"

Leaning back and crossing her long legs, Sheena shook her head. "Shit. Are you going to have any profit left over?"

"If Cruz does well, the prize money will save us."

"And getting people to support you at the highest sponsorship level." Sheena reached for the sponsorship sheets Gabriela had drawn up. "Associate sponsorship," she said.

"That will get them logos on the car and the team gear when we get some."

"For the season?"

"Yes, but they could sponsor just one race or event for less money. They can provide products. There are various sponsorship levels so that even smaller businesses can help us out."

"Wow, Gabriela, I'm impressed. How in the world did you figure all this out?"

"Filp is a genius. And so is Google?"

Sheena laughed. "Well, let's get to work. I like shopping. Let's find you and your boys a place to work. Do we need input from Flip or your driver?"

"Yeah, I'll ask Flip what kind of garage he needs and if he wants to come with us. But not from Cruz. He doesn't care about the peripheral stuff. His only interest is in driving." And in seducing her. The tenderness she'd seen in his eyes or the unmistakable attraction between them last night still made her sort of breathless. Especially the promise that a day would come when the two of them would share more than a caress beside a car.

Their little venture together was getting serious, and nowhere was there room for personal relationships or drama. Although she was glad things were changing between them and they were getting along better, she almost wished for the days when they were at each other's throats. It was safer that way—for both of them.

CHAPTER SEVEN

January

Flip chose three garage locations, all in the Inland Empire, and all had to be secure, have room enough for the car, tools, and a hauler.

"We're going to need to transport the team, too. So, we need room for a tour bus or whatever it's called," Gabriela said as she strolled through the third garage."

Flip grinned. "I usually call it a coach, but good thinking, we'll need transport from city to city."

"Why so far from L.A.?" Sheena protested.

"Cheaper," Flip said. "I like this one. What do say, Gabriela?"

"It's roomy." She looked around the empty garage. Peeking into the office, she noticed that unlike the garage, it had large windows. She could work here.

"I don't like those," Flip pointed to the windows.

"Why? That's actually what I do like about the office."

"You won't like it if people break in. Everything in this shop is going to be valuable and expensive."

The shop owner waved his arms and shook his head. "Oh no. No one is getting in here. First, they'd have to get past the welded fence perimeter, then the alarmed security system. I can install a reinforced door for the office, so even if someone did break into the office, they would not get into the shop area."

Flip eyed Gabriela, and she nodded. So, it was settled; they leased the garage in Ontario mostly because it was close to the Ontario Motor Speedway, but also, because of the security and roominess. Like Sheena said, she'd have to drive about an hour to get home every day, but who didn't have a long drive home in California?

They paid the yearly lease for the garage and spent all month moving in, and they were still not ready.

Sheena glanced at her watch. "Ready to drive back to L.A.?" Regardless of what Sheena had said about not getting involved, she drove in with Gabriela every day. They promptly decorated the office with paintings and brought in lots of indoor plants. If they had to work in a greasy garage, at least their office would look feminine and have a little class. She and Gabriela closed the remaining sponsors from the benefit dinner and got leads on additional sponsors.

Cruz took a few weeks 'off' to go visit his parents in Mexico for Christmas. Although Gabriela didn't think this was the time for him to disappear when she could use his input, she was partly relieved. Perhaps she was a coward, but she didn't want to deal with Cruz when she had so many other matters that needed to occupy her mind and time. Besides, she still wondered what had happened between the two of them the night of the sponsor dinner. Was it a simple melting of the ice or a renewal of the small fire which had only been hinted at seven years ago?

It was almost five o'clock, and the garage was still filled with people—mechanics, electricians, painters—all working to get the garage ready for the season. The new mechanics Flip hired were installing shelves and cabinets for tools. They had already completely overhauled the car. The electricians were rewiring the place to have power where they'd need it.

Gabriela sat at her desk, sifting through stacks of papers and sponsorship proposals. She had been working non-stop for hours, making phone calls and sending emails to potential sponsors. "I've got a couple more emails I need to send, then I'll be ready to go."

Despite the long hours and stress of starting a new business, she couldn't help but feel excited about their racing team.

"Good," Sheena stood by the large windows that let in plenty of light during the day. But the sun was setting, and it was getting dark. "You look exhausted."

Gabriela nodded. "I am. But I can't complain. We've done so much better than I expected. Look at all those guys we've hired and how much we've accomplished in a month."

Sheena leaned against Gabriela's desk. "Those guys have you to thank for that," Sheena said sincerely. "You've been working your butt off."

Gabriela shrugged. "So, have you, my friend."

"I'm glad you're happy because I'm staying home the rest of the week," Sheena said. "Griffin actually noticed I was gone. He said he misses me." She arched an eyebrow. "I need to let him show me how much."

"That's fine. Flip and I need to go shopping for a hauling trailer. I think we're going tomorrow."

As they spoke, a loud noise came from outside the office door, followed by a string of curses.

"What was that?" Gabriela asked, getting up from her desk.

Sheena shrugged. "I'll go check it out."

Curiosity getting the best of her, Gabriela followed Sheena into the garage.

The source of the commotion became clear when they saw Danny under a wooden shelving unit and chunks of drywall. Sheena and a couple of guys cleared the debris off him. "Are you okay?"

Danny laughed. "I guess the equipment was too heavy," he said. "The whole damned wall came down."

"Didn't I tell you?" Flip grumbled. "Now look at this mess."

"Are you sure you're okay?" Gabriela asked, frowning at Flip. The poor guy could have been killed.

Sheena helped him up, and he wrapped his arm around her waist as he stood. "I am now. Oh, wait, maybe I'm not. Keep holding on to me, Sheena baby." She laughed, and when he sat on a bench, she brushed drywall off his hair and placed her fingertips on his forehead. "You need to be careful, and you need a haircut. You're too cute to look so unkempt. And you need ice. You've got a bump growing on your forehead."

"You think I'm cute?" he grinned.

Sheena smiled. "Sure, focus on that, not the concussion you're going to have."

Gabriela rolled her eyes and pulled on Sheena's arm. "Everyone thinks you're cute, Danny. We're going home. Clean up and fix my wall. And get that ice on your head."

As they walked away, Flip said, "I think you're cute, too. Cute but stupid." Another mechanic said, "Yeah, I think you're cute, too, pretty boy."

"Shut the hell up," Danny said.

Gabriela and Sheen looked at each other and laughed. At least it wasn't boring working with a racing team.

Early the next day, Flip took her to breakfast because he said she was too skinny and didn't eat enough; then they went to buy a hauler.

"I don't know what we need," Gabriela admitted as they wandered past different trailer sizes. "I've never had to haul a car before."

"Well, I have," Flip said with a wink. "And I know exactly what we need."

He led her to the biggest trailer on the lot—a shiny black, enclosed hauling trailer with two levels and multiple compartments for tools and equipment.

Gabriela gasped when she saw the price tag. "We can't afford this."

Flip, in his calm manner, placed a hand on her shoulder. "Mira, muchacha, it'll pay for itself. It's a self-contained garage. When we're out on the road, we're going to have to take everything we need to maintain that car. Look here." He pulled her inside. "Each person will have their own locker here." He pointed to other cabinets. "Here we can store radios and headphones for when we're at the track. It has room for us to bring replacement transmissions, engines, gears," he pointed to pull-out drawers, "and other parts and pieces we'll need for the car."

It was impressive. "But Flip—."

"Trust me. You concentrate on getting us more money."

"You're spending it faster than I can get it," she said, throwing her hands up in the air.

He patted her shoulder and climbed out of the hauler, walking away.

"Flip," she sighed. "Flip, come back."

He continued to stroll toward the sales office and waved his hand in the air without slowing his pace.

Gabriela hesitated, but then she thought about all the hard work they were putting into this venture. She deserved to have the best equipment for her team, especially since they had to haul the car to about fifteen races. She followed after him. “Wait, where are you going?” she asked.

“To get us a huge discount.” He winked. “Learn how it’s done.”

Flip negotiated an amazing deal with the sales agent and, three hours later, drove off with their new car transport in tow.

Gabriela had to admit, as they pulled up to the garage where detailers were adding the names of sponsors to their car, that they were finally starting to look like a professional race team.

As they parked the hauler in the garage, the guys hurried over. “Oh man!”

Flip immediately put them to work organizing their tools and equipment inside.

Sheena walked in with a big smile on her face. “Wow, you guys are really stepping it up,” she said, admiring the trailer.

“I thought you weren’t coming in today.”

“Griffin pissed me off. He forgot that he was meeting with is video editor today. I guess he didn’t miss me as much as he said.”

“I’m sorry.”

She shrugged. “When do you think you’ll be ready for your first race? Will you need to add sponsor logos on the transporter as well.”

“We’ll be ready when the season opens in March,” Gabriela replied confidently. “And yes, if they paid for that, they’ll be added to everything.

Sheena’s eyes widened in surprise. “That’s only a few weeks away!”

“Yep, we’re pushing ourselves hard to make it happen.” Flip grinned proudly, then he gestured that Gabriela follow him.

“I’ll be in the office,” she said to Sheena.

“She can stay and help me,” Danny said. “I need her artistic eye.”

“You can have my artistic eyes, hands, and anything else you’d like, cutie.”

Gabriela couldn't help but feel grateful for Sheena's enthusiasm and support. She was quickly becoming an important part of the team. She left them laughing and acting like little kids on Christmas morning.

Flip paused when they were out of earshot of the rest of them. "Listen, I just wanted to say that, well, I'm proud of you."

"For what?

"For everything you've done for all of us."

"Ah, thank you, Flip."

He nodded. "Listen to me."

"I'm listening."

"We were all skeptical. You're just a young girl, and well, you know."

They didn't believe in her. "I know."

"But you've done your job. And now we're going to do ours. Even Cruz. I'll make sure he does."

She smiled. "Thank you, Flip."

Surprising her, he placed his hands on her shoulder, shook her a little, then leaned over and dropped a kiss on her cheek. Then he turned away with misty eyes. "I'm going to get some food. And you're going to eat lunch."

Gabriela smiled and went to the office.

When the knock came at her door, she looked up from her desk and was surprised to see Cruz standing in the doorway, looking clean and handsome in black jeans and a button-up royal blue shirt. So, he was back from Mexico. Seeing him again made her heart skip a beat.

"Is Flip around?"

"He's picking up lunch."

Cruz walked all the way inside and looked around her office. This was the first time she'd seen him since the night of the sponsor dinner. Images of them standing together beside her car rushed back and warmed her face. She could still remember the feel of his hands on her ribs, so close to her breasts. She'd wanted him to kiss her that night and had been both relieved and disappointed that he hadn't.

"He called and said he wanted to see me as soon as I got back, so here I am."

"Sit down," she said rather abruptly, irritated by her own thoughts.

Cruz continued to stand.

Was he uncooperative just to annoy her? She was the owner with the power to keep him or fire him, yet he still refused to acknowledge their positions. In fact, she wondered if his attempt at seduction in the bar that night had been his way of establishing that he was in charge. She was just a woman to him, not his boss, not the owner of a racing team. She stood. "Shall I pull out a chair for you?" She inched closer to him.

He turned his head, his attention now definitely veered from the out-of-place art prints on the walls and focused on her. He gave her a mocking look. "I'd rather stand."

Of course he would; didn't he always choose to do the opposite of what she asked? Well, if he continued to stand, so would she. Something inside her was purposely looking to antagonize him. If they returned to their old bickering ways, then maybe it would be easier to hide her attraction to him—pretend that romantic night had never happened. She leaned her backside on the desk. "Flip might be gone a while."

He shifted his position to stand right in front of her so that she could not move without running right into him. "I'll wait," he said.

As always, he used his very masculine body as a weapon. At least, that's the way it felt to her. To him, she was a female, his inferior. Or maybe he only wanted to be close to her. She lifted her chin and met his eyes. "I have work to do."

He touched her chin lightly with his index finger. "Am I keeping you from it?"

"You could wait for Flip in the garage."

“I’d rather wait in here with you.”

She felt trapped, pinned to her desk. She straightened, bringing her body flush with his, figuring he would step back. He didn’t move but instead placed his hands on her hips.

“Do you enjoy backing me into things?” she asked.

He smiled. “Yes, actually, I do.” His fingers moved up and down her hips. “Although . . . you just walked into me, didn’t you?”

“Take your hands off me, Cruz. Don’t you see how inappropriate this is?”

“I’ve been thinking—.”

“I can’t listen when you’re standing so close,” she said in a rush, then realized how that sounded.

He smiled. His hands encircled her waist. “I understand. This attraction between us is real, isn’t it?” He used his thigh to put pressure on her legs as if to open them. “I thought I’d imagined it and that when I returned, it would be gone, but the second I saw you . . . I’m not imagining it.”

“You are. Now step back.”

“We could make next season a little more fun if we just give into what we both want.”

“I explained this to you. I’m your boss. Nothing is going to happen between us.” And what happened to him not wanting to have any kind of personal relationship with her?

“Boss? No, *Querida*, you’re my owner,” he said seductively. “How does it feel to own a man?” His face brushed hers, and his lips touched her jaw below her ear.

“Come on, Cruz. Stop. This isn’t funny. Someone could come in.” But was she getting aroused? Yes, damn it. She was a woman, after all, and when he was this close, she wanted to toss all caution aside.

His fingers caressed her lower back, and his arms felt secure and right around her, as if they belonged exactly where they were. "Have you ever been kissed on top of a desk?" he asked.

But before she could answer, he captured her lips, driving her back with his upper body. She clutched his shoulders as he stretched her across the desk, and found strong, tight cords of muscle which invited a woman to follow the band down his back. His lips were hot, demanding, forceful. Her senses reeled from his forceful but artful kiss. Her lips tingled with each twist, and a pleasant ache spread across her body, a wave of delicious surrender washed over her as his hold tightened.

No longer did she have to wonder how he kissed or what he tasted like.

He cupped her backside and pulled her against the rock-hard bulge in his jeans. A different, pulsing erotic pressure now sent her tumbling through a dangerous, sensuous cloud.

Her nipples hardened instantly, and a flush covered her entire body. No one had touched her this way in over a year, maybe more, maybe never. No, no one had ever been this bold, this erotic. She began to lose control and panicked. This couldn't be happening— shouldn't be happening. She moaned to make him stop and finally rolled her head to the side. "Ohmigod, stop."

"Shh, kiss me back."

"No, I mean it, Cruz. Take your hands off me."

"Are you sure?"

"Yes."

He pushed himself off her and took her hand to help her up. He tenderly caressed her fingers. "Too uncomfortable, huh?"

She shook her head, pulled her hand from his, and placed it on her forehead to calm down. "I can't believe you just did that?" Her heart wouldn't slow. Her body was aroused to a fever pitch.

He looked baffled. "Sorry, I thought you'd enjoy—."

"You arrogant bastard." Her breath still came erratically. "You thought I'd enjoy being assaulted in my office? Don't you ever touch me again. Do you understand?" Her voice shook. She had such a mixture of emotions twirling around inside her right now that she couldn't think. Anger was her only defense.

His eyes widened. "Assault! Look, I thought . . . a few weeks ago, by your car . . . the night of the benefit dinner . . . you said you wanted me. Remember?"

She gaped at him. Unbelievable. This man was unbelievable. She didn't suppose it would help to deny she'd ever said that. "Cruz, get a clue! I deserve some respect. Even if you hate my guts, I don't deserve to be pawed at every time you see me."

His face blanched, and his eyes narrowed. He took a step back. "I didn't mean—."

"Hey, you're here." Flip cheery voice interrupted whatever Cruz was about to say.

Cruz gazed at him as if Flip were a stranger. He seemed to be in a state of shock. Was Gabriela the first woman to ever turn him down?

Flip frowned. "You two better not be fighting again."

"Flip," Gabriela said, unnerved to have him walk in while her face was probably still flushed, but relieved he hadn't arrived a few minutes earlier. "What in the world does your name mean, anyway? I've been meaning to ask you."

Flip looked at her and smiled. He glanced at Cruz once more, then sat behind Gabriela's desk, placing a paper bag from a local Mexican restaurant on top of the desk. "Felipe."

She held her hands together so they wouldn't shake. *Talk to Flip. Don't think of Cruz. Calm down.* "Felipe. I never would have guessed."

Cruz cleared his throat. "Let's take a look at the hauler, *Felipe.* I need to get the hell out of here."

Flip stood. “This thing’s amazing.” He headed out the door.

Cruz glanced at Gabriela, a heated look on his face fueled by anger, embarrassment, or passion, maybe a little of each. “I wasn’t trying to disrespect you, Miss Alende. It won’t happen again.”

She stared at him without responding. Her anger was still too raw, and she wasn’t sure who she was more upset with, him or herself, for physically reacting to his caresses and kisses so much.

“And for the record, a man can tell when a woman likes his touch.”

Their eyes remained locked. He was right. This game, the flirtation between them was real. She wanted him, and no, she hadn’t actually said the words the night of the benefit dinner, but she’d allowed him to place his hands intimately on her body, allowed him to stand so close his body heat warmed her deep inside. She’d given him the look, and he’d picked up on all of it. So, what now? Admit she was lonely, afraid, and in need of human contact? She looked away from him and shook her head. She was so confused.

His retreating footsteps alerted her that he had left. She lifted her gaze. The door slowly closed, and she caught a glimpse of Sheena and Danny in the garage laughing together. Gabriela closed her eyes. At least some people were getting along.

CHAPTER EIGHT

February

Cruz spotted the burly driver they called Sledgehammer sitting beside his car, chatting with his mechanics. The guy was a thickheaded bulldozer—when he got angry, he didn't care about his car, other driver's cars, or even his own life. He'd gotten more fines and been kicked out of more races than any other driver for his aggressive driving, but he was also the most generous with his friends.

"Guys," Cruz said as he reached Sledgehammer's garage. His race car was on a car lift—looked like it was getting a brake job.

"Well, don't you look cute," Sledgehammer said, blowing him a kiss and laughing so hard his belly shook.

For once, Cruz was clean and dressed decently. After he dropped off Sledgehammer's tax return, he would be on his way to a photo studio where Gabriela had booked the team for publicity photos.

Cruz shifted his shoulders, the crisp, white shirt scratching his neck. "I checked them over and added some deductions you could take."

"M'I gettin' money back?" He took the Manila envelope.

"Some."

Cruz wasn't an accountant yet, but every year he 'checked over' the guys' returns or simply did it for them. They reciprocated by giving him car parts, advice on car maintenance, or a few sixpacks of beer. Sledgehammer could barely read, so Cruz always did his returns first at the beginning of the year.

"A measly two-hundred and forty bucks?"

"What do you want? You didn't pay anything in?" Cruz sat on a stepladder that didn't look too dirty.

Sledgehammer grumbled and placed the envelope in a duffle bag. "Have a beer." The offer sounded like an order.

Cruz shook his head. Sledgehammer and the other three men from his team sat in the garage drinking, probably because it was the end of the night, and none of them wanted to go home. A cooler was open, and beer bottles bobbled in melting ice.

"You're not driving tonight, here." Jose, sitting beside him, said.

Cruz ignored his outstretched hand. "I'm meeting my team for a photo shoot."

They all whistled and hooted. "Gettin' fancy there, huh, Cruz?" Sledgehammer sat across from him and downed the beer left in his bottle.

"Another of Gabriela's bright ideas," Cruz said.

Sledgehammer laughed. "That's right, you got that hot babe tellin' you all what to do."

Cruz nodded. "She's the most irritating woman I've ever met. What I wouldn't give to have Carlos Alende back."

The men all grumbled and commiserated with Cruz.

"She's got you boys workin' like dogs, even durin' the holidays," Sledgehammer said, shaking his head.

"Well," Cruz shrugged. That wasn't exactly true. He had visited his parents in December for Christmas. The guys told him Gabriela had refused to let them work on the car for two weeks, even though she took no time off herself. "There's a lot to do before the start of the season."

Besides, he'd stayed out of the garage, making the guys take the car to the track so he could practice. The last thing he wanted was to run into Gabriela. He was still ticked at her for making him feel like a fool in her office. Excuse him for assuming there was something between them. Hell, maybe he'd just misread Gabriela's signals. Maybe it was wishful thinking on his part, and she had never actually shown any interest. But whether he liked it or not, she was right. She *was* his boss, and even if she was attracted to him, she probably didn't want to be. What would the other guys think if she were sleeping with the driver? He felt like shit for coming on to her like that.

"Yeah, right," Sledgehammer said. "Admit it, she's got you all on a tight leash."

"Ah, you can't blame him," Jose said with a smirk, leaning back on a pile of tires, an arm behind his head for support. "I'd jump through hoops to get into her pants too."

Cruz turned his gaze to Jose, staring, not liking his insinuation one bit. "She's my boss."

They all laughed. "Yeah."

Cruz crossed his arms. "She's a pain in the rear, but she really is working hard to get the team ready for the ARCA Menards Series West." He was surprised at how professional their team was becoming. He met Flip last week to be measured for his new fire suit. This week, he tried it on, and it had over one hundred sponsor logos. Gabriela had been busy.

"She don't know a damn thing 'bout racin'," Sledgehammer roared and pointed a finger at Cruz.

Keeping his arms crossed, Cruz brought a hand up to his chin and rubbed a bit of stubble. "She's learning." Why did he feel a need to defend her when he felt the same way most of the time?

"A woman like that has no business out here. She's not like Katie, Steve's wife, you know? Katie's been round racin' all her life. She ain't 'fraid of brakin' a nail?"

Cruz smiled, thinking of Gabriela and how delicate she actually was, even her office was full of fancy paintings and had a permanent scent of flowers. Her elegant femininity was one of the things he liked most about her. Liked her? Yeah, he really did like her, and he was proud of her.

Unexpectedly, he was grateful that nothing had happened between them. They both had more important things to concentrate on now. Race season was about to start. She'd financially outfitted them with all the essentials to run the team, and that was what mattered.

The guys had progressed to talking about their wives and everything that irritated them about them.

"That's why I don't have one," Sledgehammer said, then belched loudly.

Cruz stood and shook his head. "You don't have one because you're a slob—you have no manners."

"Oh, and you do, huh?"

"Yeah, he's a regular Casanova," Jose said.

"Go to hell," Cruz said before turning away.

"Go get 'er. Take a perty piture," they said, laughing and making kissing sounds.

Cruz made a shooing motion and continued to his car. He checked his watch, noticing he had just enough time to get to the studio. Actually, he'd be a little late . . . late enough to make Gabriela wonder. *He* wasn't jumping through hoops, no matter what the guys thought.

When he strolled into the photo studio, the rest of the team was already there, laughing and apparently having a good time. The photographer, whom Gabriela introduced as Janis, took a number of team shots immediately, then shot frames of him alone and with a mock-up of his car. She maneuvered him into so many positions that he felt like a rubber doll.

After the photographer was satisfied with his solo shots, she took a few of him shaking hands with Flip or with their arms around each other's shoulders.

"Great," Janis said. "Now, let's do a few shots with Gabriela."

From a small table where she was writing on a clipboard, Gabriela looked at them in surprise. "I'm already in the group shots. That's enough."

"You're the owner," Janis said. "You've got to have a some with your driver. Come on."

She glanced at him, and he smiled, controlling the urge to make a wisecrack about her being his owner.

The first few shots with Gabriela standing behind him went fast. He sat on a short stool. Her hands rested on his shoulders. He ignored the pleasant sensation of her hands on his body, wishing he didn't remember so clearly how great it had felt when she'd gripped his shoulder the last time.

"Okay, let's have you sitting beside each other." Janis snapped a few shots. "Good. Cruz, put one arm around her. Good. Gabriela, look into his eyes. Pretend he just won a big race. Smile. Cruz, you smile too. Great. That was a fantastic picture."

Out of the corner of his eye, Cruz saw the photographer lower the camera, but he continued to stare at Gabriela. She had beautiful eyes, and when she smiled, her entire face lit up. He wished that smile hadn't been just for the camera.

She, too, maintained eye contact for a few more seconds before turning her face. "Is that it?"

"That's it," Janis said.

Gabriela stood, picked up her clipboard again, and moved to sit on the black velvet three-step they'd used as a prop. Cruz looked over his shoulder at the guys, talking and laughing behind a partition as they changed out of their fire suits.

He followed Gabriela. "What do you intend to do with all these pictures?" he asked.

She lifted her pen from the clipboard and looked at him with a blank expression. He wondered for a second if she would answer him. Was she still angry?

"I contracted with a company that will make mugs, baseball caps, T-shirts, and other memorabilia to sell as souvenirs," she said.

"This isn't National NASCAR. You aren't going to sell very much of that kind of stuff."

She shrugged. "Oh, I don't know about that. I remember being a kid and watching people go crazy buying team souvenirs. It'll sell, particularly if you do well."

He squatted beside her and dried the perspiration on the back of his neck and jaw with a towel. "I didn't think you remembered anything about the track."

She nodded. "I remember some things." She looked tired. "The first time my dad took me to a Winston Cup race, he didn't even own a car, but it was so exciting. He bought me earplugs." Her eyes widened as if in wonderment. "But the power of those engines was so resounding I could feel the vibrations in my heart." She tapped between her breasts, and Cruz followed her hand with his eyes, noticing she, too, had a sheen of perspiration above her chest.

He wanted to wipe it for her, maybe touch her with his fingertips, absorb the moisture with his lips. He shook his head. "There's nothing like the roar of a 700 horsepower engine."

"I held on to my daddy's hand for a long time until I felt brave enough to go explore on my own."

He wondered if she realized she'd just called Carlos 'daddy.' Cruz's curiosity got the better of him. This was the first time he'd heard her speak of Carlos Alende positively. "You had a good time?"

"I was little, and it was all so thrilling."

The things Gabriela revealed about herself constantly surprised Cruz, but he was even more surprised at the emotions she created inside him. He wondered who she talked to about things that mattered to her. Maybe Sheena. A sudden rush of envy made him wish she'd confide in him instead. She had no parents and no siblings. How lonely she must be. He spoke with his parents on the phone every week, and he had lots of extended relatives in the L.A. area. A person needed family.

He looked down at the tip of his shoe, not knowing what to say to her. "These fire suits look great, by the way."

Her face brightened. "Don't they?"

He nodded. "Looks like you've gotten lots of sponsors."

"I have. How do you think I'm paying for the trailer and garage, or the rest of it?"

"So, are we going to be all set up to start the season? We're only about a month away, you know?"

"I'm ready. The car's ready. How about you? Flip told me you haven't been practicing much."

He shrugged. Flip needed to mind his own business. He had practiced enough. "With that souped-up car and this great suit, how could I not be ready?"

Janis returned and stood beside Cruz. Gabriela smiled and got to her feet. "Ready?" She asked.

Janis nodded. "I've got everything put away."

"Great." Gabriela turned to him. "We're going to dinner." Then, almost as an afterthought, she added. "Want to come?"

Did he want to go out to dinner with two beautiful women? Of course, but . . . "Do you two know each other?"

"We went to art school together. I knew she was fantastic," Gabriela said. "And she gave us a great price."

"I see," Cruz stood. "I'm gonna pass." Gabriela had been sitting on that step, waiting for a friend. And he'd thought she was sitting all alone because she was lonely. He was a fool. Why would a woman like Gabriela need to talk to him?

"Are you sure, Cruz?" Janis smiled. "Gabriela gets to spend time with sexy race car drivers all the time, but I don't."

Gabriela wasn't impressed by fast cars or fast men. Cruz glanced at her, and a crazy sense of shame warmed his face. How could he have been so stupid to make a pass at her on top of her desk? He'd gotten so used to sleeping with cheap groupie women who hung out at the track that he'd forgotten how to be a gentleman. He'd been brought up to be respectful and honorable, yet he'd managed to be just the opposite every time he was with Gabriela. Somehow, he'd make it up to her. "You're not missing much," he said to Janis. "Give me a second to get out of this suit and I'll get out of your way."

After he had changed into his street clothes, he followed them outside. While Gabriela's friend locked the studio, they strolled to her car.

"Hey, Gabriela. I'm sorry, you know, about what I did in your office."

She gazed at him, then finally gifted him with a soft smile. "Me too."

"You have nothing to be sorry for. It was me." He gave her a lopsided grin. "I've been hanging around men for too long. And none of us are too far removed from cavemen."

She smiled. He chuckled.

When Janis returned, he watched them climb into Gabriela's car and leave. He shoved his hands in his pockets.

As he observed the jumble of cars down the street, he rubbed the middle of his chest with the heel of his hand. Something told him he wasn't all that off about Gabriela being a lonely woman. The cold, aloof manner and take-charge attitude were survival mechanisms. A way to ward off painful emotions.

Or maybe . . . he was just full of crap.

CHAPTER NINE

March

Cruz loaded his bags into the bottom of the RV coach, then leaned on his car to smoke a cigarette while he waited for Gabriela and Danny to show up for their first trip—their first race. The rest of the team had already arrived and stood beside the garage, talking among themselves. The sun was sinking lower, painting the horizon with its final, warm glow.

For just a moment, he drew in a breath to mentally prepare himself. He had quit his job, hadn't re-enrolled in his college classes for the year, and was about to embark on a season of racing unlike any he'd experienced before.

He remembered when Carlos Alende told him they were moving from the local city races to the Southwest Featherlight; the excitement he'd felt had barely allowed him to sleep. Well, that was nothing compared to the caliber of racing he'd be driving in now.

Yet, he didn't feel the same type of nervous excitement he had then. Maybe because Carlos Alende wasn't with them. After all, it was his car they were racing. But no, that wasn't the real reason, and he knew it. With Carlos, racing had been fun. Win or lose, it really didn't matter. But with

Gabriela, it mattered. Their future was riding on how well Cruz drove. This was for real, and what he actually felt was fear.

He saw Gabriela's car pull into the parking lot. A few moments later, she got out, and three of the guys jumped to help her load her bags into the trailer. She sure as hell didn't have a problem getting male attention. That bothered him more than he cared to admit. Not that she noticed how men gawked at her, and she certainly didn't know the suggestive things they said when she wasn't around. Although the men on his team were well-behaved. He took one more puff and flicked the cigarette away. He eased away from his car. She glanced at him and smiled. His heart beat a little quicker.

"Hello, Cruz."

He blew smoke out the side of his mouth so it wouldn't touch her. "We've been waiting for you for thirty minutes." Damn, he sounded like he was criticizing her. From the look in her eyes, he could tell she thought so, too.

"Sorry. We can go now."

"Danny's late too, so no, we can't go."

"I'll wait in the coach."

"Suit yourself. I'll have another cigarette."

She took a couple of steps toward the coach, then stopped and turned back to him. "You smoke?"

"Now and then. That a problem?"

She shook her head. "It's your life." She continued toward the coach.

Cruz took another cigarette from the package in his shirt pocket, and as he lit it, he leaned on his car again. He released a cloud of smoke and saw Gabriela making herself comfortable inside their traveling home. He didn't get it. The picture her father had painted of her and the real woman didn't jibe.

Supposedly, she had constant wild parties that included alcohol, drugs, you name it. But so far, he'd taken her to a bar where she'd ordered coffee, and now she was obviously bothered by his smoking. And she hadn't jumped into bed with him the first chance she got. She sure didn't seem like the wild teenager of three or four years back. Was this a magical transformation, or had the old man been wrong? People didn't change that much, and he'd be willing to bet his career that Gabriela Alende was no party animal.

He dropped the cigarette and ground it out with the ball of his shoe. Opening his car door, he tossed the pack inside, deciding not to smoke on this tour. As he walked toward the coach, he told himself he wanted to quit anyway. He wasn't doing this to please Gabriela. He didn't care what she thought.

Cruz climbed inside and walked past Gabriela, who'd sat on a couch behind the driver captain's chair. She stared out of the window, looking sad and alone. Was she as worried as he about this first race? Her future was riding on the outcome as much as his. Beside the small kitchen counter, he paused and pulled out a thermos of coffee from his backpack, filling two Styrofoam cups. He walked back down the aisle.

"Here."

She glanced at him, then straightened and took the cup. "Thanks."

He shrugged. "We've got a long ride to Arizona."

She nodded.

"If you get lonely, I'll be in the back."

She stared at him, large brown eyes filled with questions. "I'll be fine."

Yes, she would be. She was a survivor, a tough young woman. He smiled. "If I get lonely, can I come see you?"

The corners of her lips lifted a little. "You'll be fine, too."

He nodded. Then leaned forward and touched her shoulder. "I'm going to do okay on the qualifying run. Don't worry, okay?"

She glanced at his hand, then looked him in the eyes. "I'm not worried. You're going to do great, Cruz. I know it."

Why did her confidence in him surprise him? Every time she made a statement like that, he was taken aback. It felt good to have someone encouraging him, believing in him. He hadn't realized how tense his back muscles were until now. He let her shoulder go. "Yeah."

"If you need anything, let me know," she said. "It's my job to make sure your needs are met on this trip."

Was it? As the team owner, none of the day-to-day chores were her responsibility. Did she know that? But if she wanted to take care of his needs . . . he needed to sit beside her, hold her hand, stare into her eyes. She made him feel good. He swallowed. "Sure thing."

Danny finally arrived. Gabriela's friend, Sheena, dropped him off. Cruz had seen her helping Gabriela out in the office but hadn't paid much attention to her. Apparently, Danny had. The rest of the men were boarding the motorcoach, so he didn't explore where his thoughts were taking him any further. He returned to the back, sat on a narrow bunk, and soon was joined by most of the guys except Flip, who eased into the driver's seat.

They rode most of the way in those positions. The men played cards on the little kitchen table. Gabriela either read or slept, and didn't talk to anyone except Flip. Cruz tried to rest and not think of the coming race, or of how lovely Gabriela's lips were when she slept. From the back, he noticed they were slightly parted, full, and red. Part of him wanted to move closer and see just how soft and moist they might be, but he closed his eyes instead. He wouldn't be kissing those lips ever again, so his best bet was to stop looking.

Danny sat beside him. "Sorry, I was late."

"No problem."

"I woke up to a damned flat tire."

"Mm, that's why Sheena dropped you off?"

"Yeah, I didn't want to fix it this morning. She was cool enough to hurry over."

Cruz nodded and gazed at him. Did the kid realize that woman was way out of his league? Pretty much like Gabriela was for him. "Definitely nice of her."

"She said she didn't mind. Gabriela asked her to do some paperwork, promo stuff, so she had to go to the office. Anyway, just wanted to say sorry. Didn't want you to think I was fucking around, sleeping in and taking my sweet time getting to the garage."

"I would never think that," Cruz held up his fist, and they bumped knuckles. "It's all good."

They reached Phoenix, Arizona around midnight, and pulled into the hotel parking lot where Gabriela had booked rooms for the next four days. The guys climbed off, stretching and yawning.

"She still asleep?" Cruz asked Flip as he walked down the aisle. He stared at her. She looked like a fragile angel.

"Yeah."

"You need to wake her. We're here."

Flip took a step back. "Why me?"

"Aren't you first in command here?"

Flip frowned.

"Go check everyone in, Flip," Cruz said, his voice sounding tired even to him.

"What about her?"

"Go on out. I'll wake her."

Flip nodded and left. Cruz sat beside Gabriela and watched her for a few moments. Her chest rose and fell with each deep breath. A warm, content feeling filled his chest. Watching a woman sleep was one of life's greatest pleasures. He didn't want to wake her. He went to the back of the trailer and pulled a blanket off the double bed, then returned and placed it over her. She moaned and cuddled into the warm cotton. Cruz smiled.

He sat across from her, leaned back on the swiveling captain's chair, and lifted his legs over the other seats. He crossed his arms to keep himself warm. After watching Gabriela for almost an hour, he closed his eyes and went to sleep.

The coach had stopped moving, and out the window, Gabriela saw nothing but darkness, except for a pink neon motel sign, flashing at regular intervals. She straightened and noticed Cruz across the aisle from her, sleeping. No one else was on the coach. She pushed the blanket off her shoulders, wondering where it had come from.

Cruz opened his eyes. "It's cold. Keep it on."

"Where is everyone?"

"Probably nice and warm in their rooms."

"When did we get here?"

"Last night sometime."

Gabriela looked at her watch, shocked that it was four in the morning. She stretched. "Why didn't you wake me?"

He shrugged. "You looked comfortable."

His arms were tightly crossed, and he was pressed against the seat. "You don't."

"I'm cold."

"Here." She offered him the blanket.

He lowered his legs, stood, then crossed the aisle. "Move over."

"What?"

"Let me sit by you."

She slid to one side of the couch, and he sat beside her. She felt closed in, but pleasantly trapped.

He took the blanket and repositioned it so it covered both their upper bodies. He leaned into her. "This way, we can keep each other warm."

"Cruz—."

Over the blanket, he rested a hand on her belly, and though it seemed innocent enough, she still jumped.

"Are you hungry?" he asked.

"No," she whispered, forgetting to breathe.

"The guys left chips and dip, and—."

"I'm not hungry," she said in a rush.

His hand slid slowly to her rib cage, pulling her closer, snuggling in as if she were his personal teddy bear. "We can have a big breakfast in a couple of hours."

She nodded. "Great."

"Try to get more sleep." He closed his eyes.

She wouldn't be able to sleep. Not with Cruz so close. Was he ever going to take his hand off her? She could ask him to, but the intimacy of their "sleeping arrangement" didn't seem to affect him in the slightest. Pretty soon, he'd start snoring. She gazed at his handsome face, free of tension and relaxed. His head rested on the seat, angled toward her. She took her time noticing how his eyelashes touched the skin below, almost coming in contact with his high cheekbones. His morning beard was coming in and it would probably feel like fine gravel under her fingertips if she ran them over his face. And his lips. Oh God. She closed her eyes and shifted her body. Her shoulder touched his, and she knew she had to say something. "I don't think the guys should come in here and find us sleeping together, like . . . well, like this."

"Mm?" He tightened his fingers around her side for a moment, then pulled his hand away. "You're right. There's a bed in the back. You can use that if you want, and I'll stretch out here on the couch."

The last thing she wanted was to get near that bed. Not that she didn't trust him, but just the idea made her nervous. "No, I guess this is fine, after all."

He rested his head back and closed his eyes again. Their shoulders continued to touch. Gabriela was aware of every breath he took, every twitch of every muscle. Cruz seemed to be all muscle. Strong, sexy, handsome, all man. The skinny kid she'd been infatuated with when she was seventeen was like a different person. This harsh man beside her awakened dark, sensual passions and made her want to cross the line.

"You cut your hair," he said, his voice deep and rumbly, his eyes still closed.

She didn't look at him. Was he sitting there thinking of her as well? "A little."

"It looks nice."

"Thanks."

He twisted his body and bent his head, so she had to look into his now open eyes. "Everything about you looks nice. You turn heads anytime you enter a room."

She shuddered as if he'd touched her.

"That day in your office—."

"I told you to forget it."

He shook his head. "You put me in my place. I deserved it. You're my boss, and—."

"Cruz, please." She had been partly to blame, and more tempted and turned on than she should have been. He'd said a man knew when a woman was interested, and he'd known exactly how much she'd craved his touch. "Maybe I gave you mixed messages. Maybe you were too pushy and aggressive. We were both wrong. Let's agree to move past it."

"Okay. But first, why do you say you gave me mixed messages?"

"I don't want to talk about this.

"I do. I'm attracted to you, but I shouldn't have acted on it. I admit it. Why can't you?"

Admit that she was attracted to him? No. First, he already knew that, and second, if she said it, if she gave him any indication of how much she wanted him, it would encourage him to pursue what they both wanted. She simply shook her head.

"Fine, I have one more question," he said.

"What?" she whispered in the quiet coach.

"Under different circumstances . . . ." He stopped and looked away from her. "Do you think you and I could have been . . .?"

Could have been friends? Could have been lovers? Was he going to finish his sentence or make her wonder forever? She touched his chin, and his eyes returned to her face.

"Cruz, the only circumstances I know about are the ones we're living in now. Our relationship is pretty clear."

His gaze lowered to her lips. "You're the owner of a race team, and I'm the driver."

"Yes."

"Is that all you want? I could be so much more for you."

Her whole body suddenly grew warm, and every cell was alive, anticipating, wanting. Who was she fooling? It didn't matter that she owned the team and he was the driver. He was a man, and she a woman, and they both knew they wanted each other. How long would they be able to continue ignoring the pull between them? She forced herself to drop her hand from his chin before something happened that would be impossible to stop this time. "I want our team to succeed. That's all I want."

He sighed heavily and eased away from her.

She wanted to say more, to admit she was attracted to him too, but to what end? "No, that's not all I want. I want us to be friends," she said. "Maybe we already are."

"I think I'll take that bed." He stood. "Couch is all yours, friend."

The guys unloaded the race car from the trailer. Both mechanics prepared to make last-minute adjustments before Cruz's test runs. Gabriela sat on the coach on her cell phone, ordering lunch for the team, trying to stay out of their way. She'd learned in the past months how irritated men got when they were being questioned or watched. She also found that by appearing only when something was important, everyone listened and followed her suggestions.

Out of the coach window, she watched Cruz pace beside the car, pat his left shirt pocket as if he were going to pull a cigarette pack out, then finally turn and disappear into the track area.

From their qualifying runs today, the drivers would get their starting positions. This was their first race in the Western division—what they'd worked so hard for the past few months. Everyone was nervous.

Climbing out of the coach, she went after Cruz. She found him leaning against the low wall in the pit area, watching other drivers make their runs. She leaned on the wall beside him. He glanced at her for an instant, then returned his attention to the track.

"I bet you can't wait to get out there and get a feel for the track," she said, knowing he must have an incredible amount of anxiety.

"Hmm," he seemed to agree. He continued to stare at the track. "See that third curve?"

"Yes." The warm sun touched her face, creating a pleasant and relaxed sensation on an otherwise anxious day.

"See how the cars have a tendency to head towards the outside?" Cruz leaned closer to her and pointed.

"Yeah, they get close to the wall."

"Right, and I tend to turn wide, anyway. I've got to make sure I make a very tight turn there."

She slanted her head and watched his strong chin and determined facial features. "That's a good observation."

"Looks like there's an angle, too."

"There is. I read the specs for the track. There's a twenty-degree angle on the bank coming out of the curve."

He looked at her. "Twenty degrees?"

"Yep."

He smiled and continued to stare at her. Then his smile faded. "This is it, Gabriela. I either get a good starting position, or it's over before it starts."

She placed a hand on his forearm. "You're an amazing driver. Don't worry. All you have to do is finish the race."

He nodded. "I better go see if the car is ready."

"Right," she said, dropping her hand from his arm.

He stepped away, but before he turned to walk down the ramp to the garage, he stopped. "Remember when I said I didn't care if you made any money at this or not?"

How could she forget? He'd been so cold and cruel, and he'd told her exactly how little he'd thought of her. She'd seen the disgust in his eyes. Gabriela swallowed the pain that mounted inside and settled in her throat. "I remember."

"It was a rotten thing for me to say. I'm going to do the best I can out there for you—for all of us. I just wanted you to know that." He turned and disappeared.

Gabriela stayed where she was, feeling like he'd given her a precious gift. To know that she and Cruz were working toward the same goal and that they'd be able to start this season with some of that animosity suspended filled her with relief and happiness. A few minutes later, she watched car number 58 enter the track and tear around the speedway. She prayed he would have a good qualifying run.

Cruz not only did fantastic qualifying, starting in the third position from the pole, but got everyone's attention when, on race day, he took the number two spot. Who was this rookie who came out of nowhere? Gabriela and Flip were interviewed by the local Phoenix papers, radio, and T.V. news stations. Cruz looked overwhelmed when questioned, but was charming and amazingly articulate.

By the time they had finished loading the car into the trailer, it was close to one A.M., but everyone was too wound to sleep.

"Let's go get a drink," Flip suggested.

The crew had already opened a few six-packs in the coach. More drinking didn't sound appealing. "I'm going to turn in," Gabriela said.

Cruz's wide smile tapered. "Why don't you come with us?"

She shook her head. Having spent every minute of every day with these men, she needed the nights to be hers. "You all have a good time." She grabbed her jacket, her backpack full of her notes, and her laptop.

A couple of other guys protested, and Cruz stepped forward. He reached for her backpack and eased her fingers loose. "You've got to come with us," he said in a low voice, meant only for her ears. "The team deserves a celebration, don't you think?"

She met his eyes. They sparkled with happiness and friendship. His whole demeanor toward her had changed lately. He seemed barely able to hold his enthusiasm in check. The man definitely deserved a celebration after the race he'd run. She looked away from his challenging eyes. "Only for one drink. I'm tired," she said, loud enough for the others to hear.

Everyone cheered and climbed into the coach, talking among themselves now that the decision had been made. They drove to a small country-western bar where they claimed three tables. The guys pushed them together with ease and, after ordering their drinks, began discussing the race blow by blow. Cruz described his trembling hands, the new speeds he had introduced the car to, and his stomach burning from nerves. The pit crew boasted, with obvious satisfaction, how smoothly the stops went. Everything seemed to go their way. Flip, the mechanics, everyone had given it their all. Gabriela watched her team, and an unfamiliar feeling swelled in her heart—a mixture of affection and pride.

"And Gabriela." Flip patted her shoulder in a tender, fatherly manner.

She lifted her eyes, leaving her own thoughts behind with a smile, bringing her attention to what he was saying.

"You've put this all together. To Gabriela." He lifted his glass, and the others joined him.

Gabriela lifted her own glass. "Thank you. To the rest of the season." They all echoed her words. She met Cruz's sexy, half-closed eyes. He touched his glass to hers and winked.

As he watched her sip her drink, Cruz wanted to run his tongue along her wet upper lip. The woman turned him on; there was no escaping it. He reached across and took her hand. "Let's dance."

She looked startled but allowed him to lead her to the dance floor, where couples slowly moved to the melodic twang of a lonesome song.

He pulled her close, reminding himself that he promised to behave. A gentleman, he would be a gentleman. "Can I admit something to you?"

She nodded, her face close to his.

"I was so scared today."

Her sleepy eyes watched him for a few long seconds as they moved together easily. "Me too," she said finally. "But I was confident you'd do well."

They stared into each other's eyes, silently ending their antagonism, or so it seemed to him. He didn't hate her anymore for how she had treated Carlos Alende. Maybe it was disloyal of him, but far from hating, he liked Gabriela and admired her. And God help him, he wanted her. "What did you have to be afraid of?" he asked.

She shrugged, her body flush against his. "That we wouldn't be able to pull it off. That everyone would find out what a fraud I really am. That I'm just a woman with an art degree that has no business on a track with guys like you." She paused and set the side of her face against his. "That's just for starters. What were you afraid of?"

He tightened his hold on her, wanting to tell her she belonged right alongside them. She'd worked just as hard, deserved just as much credit. But he decided to answer her question instead. "That I'd blow it. That I'd let you and Flip and the guys down. That I'd be the last one to cross the finish line."

They glided together until the song ended. Then he reluctantly eased back from her, and she did the same. Having held on to each other and absorbed a bit of comfort gave them each the strength to return to the table. But neither did.

"I'll never tell," she said. "No one will ever know how we really felt. It'll be our secret."

He nodded, wondering about the double meaning of her words. Would all the stupid things he'd said and done to her be their secret, too? "Thank you. Do you want to dance some more?"

She shook her head. "I want to finish my drink with the guys."

Early the next morning, the crew boarded the coach. Unaccustomed to drinking, Gabriela had a terrible hangover. She'd had three drinks. The men didn't seem to notice. The coach was filled with a charged aura, a feeling that maybe they would be able to survive in the Western Regionals after all.

For the first time, Gabriela knew they would not just survive but excel in the series. What she didn't know was how she'd continue to travel with Cruz and not admit that she was falling for him. She rode all the way home without speaking to him. For most of the trip, she slept or pretended to sleep. Cruz didn't attempt to talk to her. When they returned to their lot in California, they went their separate ways without even saying goodbye. Maybe he realized she needed space. Maybe he did as well.

CHAPTER TEN

April

Gabriela designed posters of their first race. She obtained digital pictures from the track photographer and uploaded them into the computer. Then she put her artistic talents to work and created a fabulous promotional poster. She carried one out to the garage and hung it on the wall over the mechanic's workbench. Standing back, she held her hair off her neck, trying to cool off in the warm, sticky garage. As she studied it, she made a mental list of who she would send the posters to, for sure to all the potential sponsors who were still sitting on the fence.

She especially liked the picture of Cruz climbing out of his car. The triumphant look on his face was worth a million bucks. Yes, this poster was . . . perfect. She headed to the storage room to get more ink for her printer.

For once, the garage was quiet. No one was working on the car today. She opened the door and heard a gasp. As her eyes adjusted to the darkness, she saw two people, Sheena and Danny, scrambling. Sheena's blouse hung open, and she was half reclined over boxes. Danny leaned over her. Both were flushed.

"Gabriela," Sheena said and pushed Danny away.

"Uh, sorry," Gabriela mumbled, closed the door and turned away.

In her haste to leave the scene, she ran right into Cruz's hard chest. His hands firmly gripped her upper arms. "Hey, where are you going in such a hurry?"

"Cruz. Sorry," she repeated. "Um, to my office, I guess."

He smiled. "Good. I was coming to see you."

She eased out of his grip. "Really? What about?"

He pointed toward her office. "I'll follow you."

"Right." She glanced at the storage room. Sheena and Danny? How long had that been going on? Why hadn't she said anything? What about Griffin?

She gathered the posters from her desk and placed them in a box.

Cruz stood behind her and looked over her shoulder. "Wow. Nice. I'm a handsome devil, aren't I?" He grinned.

His breath touched her ear; his voice was soft and smooth. She moved past him, still flustered over seeing Shenna in the closet with Danny. What the hell was she thinking? "That you are. What did you want to talk to me about?"

He took one of the posters out of the box. "What are you going to do with the posters?"

A moment ago, she'd been so excited about the way the posters turned out; now, Sheena had distracted her. "They're for the sponsors to thank them for supporting us. It also keeps them informed on how well you're doing."

He nodded. "Are you sure you didn't earn a marketing degree?"

Sheena pushed the door open and burst into the room. "I can explain," she called out. Both Cruz and Gabriela turned around to look at her. But when Sheena saw Cruz, she stopped.

"Oh, Cruz. Hi."

He parted his lips as if he were going to answer, but Gabriela snapped the poster out of his hand. “Why *are* you here? You still haven’t told me.”

“Well.” He frowned. “Next week’s race is in Bakersfield, which is one of my old tracks. We raced there often with your dad, and . . . I know a lot of the fans.”

She sat behind her desk, crossed her legs, and shrugged. “So?”

“Mind if we display the car before the race? Give fans a chance to check it out and talk to us?”

Seemed like a great idea to her. Publicity was always good. “I don’t mind at all. Have you set it up with the track owner?”

He shook his head. “Flip did.”

“Oh.” So why ask her if the decision had been made? “Fine.”

He placed his hands on his hips, nodded, then glanced back at Sheena again. He leaned toward her desk. “Everything okay?”

“Sure. Good idea on displaying the car. I’ll add that to the day’s events.”

He nodded. “Okay. I’ll see you later then.” He walked past Sheena on his way out, waving goodbye.

Gabriela stared at Sheena. “Well?”

Sheena smiled. “Are you angry?”

“He’s part of the pit crew and super young. What are you doing?”

“Just having some fun.” Sheena stepped further into the room and sat on a corner of her desk. “He’s so cute.”

Danny *was* cute. Blond, blue eyes, baby face, sweet. “How long have you two been doing whatever you’re doing?”

“Nothing is going on." Sheena smiled. "Yet.”

“From what I saw, something *is* going on. And in a closet, really?”

She hopped off the desk. “I didn’t think you’d be upset—.”

“I’m not upset.” But she was. Why? Was it because she’d thought of being in the same position with Cruz? And that scared her?

Sheena stared at her with a slight smirk. She knew Gabriela too well.

"I just don't want anyone to get hurt." That much was true. Sheena could be a bit of a snob. She'd never take a relationship with someone like Danny seriously. And she wouldn't think twice about breaking his heart. Gabriela didn't want that to happen. She liked Danny, cared about him, cared about all of them. This was her team, and more than once, they'd been there to help her. Whether it was to put together the closet organizer, put air in her tires, or simply walk her to her car late at night, all the guys, even Cruz, went out of their way for her. "You're engaged to someone else. Leading Danny on is cruel."

Sheena laughed. "Leading him on? He's having fun, and so am I. You think he's interested in something serious with me?"

Gabriela's gaze sharpened, and her posture stiffened. "Griffin is. What do you think he'd say about you having fun with another guy?"

"He'd be pissed, so he's never going to find out." Sheena lifted an eyebrow and strolled to the window, leaning casually on the sill. "You know I'm not married yet, right?"

Really, what Sheena did was none of her business, but she was disappointed. "Maybe you don't want to be, Sheena. It's okay to call it off," she said softly, her voice carrying a note of gentle sympathy.

With a brisk motion, Sheena picked up a stack of posters from Gabriela's desk and offered a distracted smile. "Should I help you put these into the canisters so we can mail them?" She asked, then paused and shot a glance back with a shake of her head. "I'm not calling it off. Griffin perfect. My parents like him. He's going to be massively successful one day. He's the right guy for me."

"Don't sleep with Danny, then."

With a casual shrug and a mischievous grin, she said, "Too late."

"Oh Sheena. You just told me nothing is going on.

"Nothing is. He's fun and into me, and I need something uncomplicated and immature, and a little wicked. We spend hours laughing, playing video games, drinking frappuccinos, and having sex until we pass out. You don't know how liberating it is to be with someone who isn't obsessed with his career."

Gabriela couldn't relate. She was definitely obsessed with her business. Maybe she was too serious, but maybe she just had more to lose. Sheena had her family, and they would love her no matter what. "So, on the one hand, you love Griffin because he's going to be *massively successful* because he *is* obsessed over his career, but on the other, that's sending you into some other guy's bed? Do you hear how screwed up that is?"

"Gabby, don't."

"Don't what?"

"Don't do this. Just be my friend."

"Fine. As long as Danny knows about Griffin and that you're not serious about him, I guess you're both adults."

"I didn't say he knows about Griffin. We don't talk about stuff."

Wonderful. She hoped this didn't all blow up in Sheena's face. "Whatever. Let's get to work. Go ahead and put the posters into the canisters."

The glow from the Las Vegas strip was visible from the middle of the desert, looking like the earth had opened up and exposed its flaming center. As they descended into the valley, enormous hotels came into view, and dazzling lights twinkled in every color of the rainbow.

Everyone on the coach moved to the window, ooing and aweing. Everyone except Flip.

Gabriela grabbed his collar and shook. "This is awesome, Flip. Aren't you excited?"

He shrugged. “I’ve been coming to Vegas since before you were born. It was better before all the glitter.”

She stared out the window, kneeling on the seat. “I can’t imagine it looking better than this!”

He glanced over his shoulder. “When I was a young man, that’s when Vegas was great. You could eat for less than a buck, smoke all you wanted, hotels were cheap, and there weren’t any kids running around. Now they’ve made the place into Disneyland, dancing water and shit. Aah.” He waved a hand in disgust and leaned his head back. He closed his eyes.

Gabriela smiled and continued to stare out the window. She would have loved to come here with her college friends. For the next forty-five minutes, she watched the city get closer and closer until they pulled up to their hotel. Gabriela checked them all in, and didn’t see any of the guys the rest of the night.

She spent the first night alone, strolled through the casinos, stopping at slot machines here and there, unable to resist their ringing bells and twinkling lights. After losing a couple of twenties, she sat at a bar to watch a band and sip a glass of wine. The wine warmed and relaxed her. A small part of her wished she had someone to share all this glamour with. Once upon a time, it would have been Sheena, but she did *not* travel with them to any of the races, and she was glad. She was spending the weekend with Griffin, her perfect man who paid so little attention to her that it broke Gabriela’s heart. Maybe things would work out for them, but maybe it wouldn’t be so bad if they didn’t.

She swirled the wine in her glass, and Cruz came to mind only for an instant. Of course, he was the last person she should share a glass of wine and some soft music with. It wasn’t his style, anyway. The closest he’d gotten to being sentimental and communicative had been in the country western bar in Arizona when they’d shared that dance. That night, she’d wished she could close her eyes and stay in his arms forever.

But she and Cruz were too different. The best thing they could hope for was friendship, which actually seemed to be developing rather well lately. She took another sip of wine, but it failed to warm her heart.

🏁

The next morning, Cruz ran his practice and qualifying run. Afterward, for the first time ever, none of the guys hung out at the track. As soon as the car was checked and locked in the garage, they were gone. Gabriela was the only one who waited for Cruz after he parked the car in the garage and changed his clothes.

"Looks like you'll have a good start tomorrow," she said, handing him a bottle of water as he walked out of the trailer.

He grinned and raised his hands to the sky. "Can you believe this? It's unbelievable."

He'd won the Bakersfield race, and the possibilities were good for this one. "You've got a good chance of moving into first place."

"I know it." He finally took the water from her. "It's amazing. I feel like I'm in a dream."

"It's real."

He looked around. "Where's Danny?"

"Everyone's gone."

He laughed. "Yeah, I figured as much. Flip was probably the first one out."

"Oh yes. All that talk about how Vegas has changed and about how he doesn't care for it anymore didn't keep him from shooting out of here the second you crossed the finish line and got your time."

"Tomorrow's his birthday, you know."

She shook her head. "I didn't."

He began walking, and she fell into step beside him.

"I have a gift for him in the coach. I didn't take it out because we're bunking in the same room, and I don't have anywhere to hide it. It's not wrapped. I was wondering if. . . ." He angled his head and narrowed his eyes as he looked at her.

"What?"

"Can I stash it in your room?"

"Of course."

They stopped by the trailer. "You gonna be in your room tonight?"

She wanted to catch a show. "I don't know. I'll tell you what, I'll give you my extra key. Just stop by and leave the gift in there." She pulled the key from her bag and gave it to him.

He took the credit-card-like key from her slender fingers and slipped it into his shirt pocket. "Thanks."

"No problem, just leave the key in my room when you leave."

He leaned on the trailer, his ankles crossed, and watched her climb the steps to the track office. He took her room key from his pocket and ran his fingers across the smooth plastic. That old fantasy of Gabriela and himself wrapped together in bed was still alive inside him. What he wouldn't give to have her hand over her room key with more in mind than him dropping off a gift. Being with her so much on the road, in the garage, early morning breakfasts and late-night dinners . . . all of it just served to draw him closer and fuel his imagination. He tucked the key away again. His imagination was all he'd have. She'd made that perfectly clear. She wasn't interested in him.

She was polite, kind, and never argued with him anymore, maybe because he wasn't in her face. But Gabriela Alende still had one goal—make as much money as possible so she could leave racing and all of them. Someday, she'd probably look back on all this as a terrible nightmare she'd had to endure to get her life back. And he'd remember it as some of the best times of his life.

Cruz held Flip's gift in one hand and inserted the key into the door slot with the other. A green light blinked, and he pushed the door open. Only one lamp was on, but it was enough to see. He walked inside and dropped the box on one of the double beds.

He turned to leave, looked up, and heard water running right before he saw Gabriela through a smoky glass wall that separated the bathroom from the bedroom.

Standing under the shower, she lathered soap on her chest, abdomen, and legs. Then she turned around, her head was thrown back, allowing water to spray on her hair and long, sleek body. Foamy white bubbles slid down her ribs and over her hips. Water droplets ran down her full breasts, dripping off the pointed tips.

Cruz tried to move, but his legs wouldn't budge. The breath in his lungs burned as he failed to exhale. He stared through the glass at her naked body, his jaw slack. The glass distorted specific details, but he could still see her curved, womanly shape clearly. His attention moved to the darkness at the apex of her legs, and his own body hardened. With the bathroom light shining brightly, it looked like a spotlight was on her. She was beautiful, simply perfect.

He shook his head, knowing he had to get out of there before she saw him, but the only part of his body that seemed to be working was inside his jeans, growing and hardening.

Then suddenly, the water turned off, and she was reaching for a towel. Cruz, looked around the room for a place to hide. He grabbed the box quickly and headed for the door. Just as he got there, he felt more than saw the steam coming from the bathroom.

Quickly, he knocked on the inside of the door. "Hello."

She gasped and turned around, clutching her towel around her breasts.

"Hey, it's only me," he blurted.

"Cruz?"

"I thought you weren't going to be here?" he asked.

"I'm not. I came to shower and change before going out. She had backed herself against the wall, pasted herself against it with the towel held tight to her chest.

"I brought the gift. Can I set it on the bed?"

"On the bed?"

He nodded and pointed. "I'll put it right there and leave so you can finish getting ready." He couldn't believe he was managing to speak, walk, and act like he hadn't just about had an orgasm watching her lush, wet body.

"Just a minute." She disappeared into the bathroom and came out a few seconds later wearing a robe. "What did you buy him?"

Cruz smiled, relieved that she'd covered up, trying to get the image of her behind that glass out of his mind. "Want to see?"

She nodded.

His hands shook as he opened the lid of the rectangle box. From inside, he pulled out a lacquered classical guitar. "The last time I went to Mexico, I picked one up."

"Does Flip play?"

Cruz half grinned. "You might call it that. He likes to sing old Spanish melancholic songs while he thinks of all his lost loves."

Gabriela gave him a soft smile. Cruz couldn't pull his gaze off her. He wanted to lay her on the bed beside them and slowly pull that robe off, touch that gorgeous body he'd gotten a peek at, stretch his own naked body over hers, and feel her soft skin against his own. He could almost feel her legs around his hips as he gradually entered her, and she urged him deeper until he'd filled her completely.

"Maybe you should give it to him with the condition that he can't bring it on tour with us," she said.

Cruz nodded and pressed his lips together, trying to get a grip. He returned the guitar to the box. "Tomorrow, after the race, I told him I'd take him to dinner. I'll come back and get it then if it's okay."

She crossed her arms, looking relaxed, clean, beautiful. "Sure, I'll be here."

He stuck his hands in his pockets and took a step backward. "I appreciate it." He turned to leave.

"Oh, Cruz, my key."

"Right," he said and reached into his back pocket to pull it out.

"Thanks," she said as she took it. "Don't want you walking in again."

If she only knew. He shrugged. "You look cute, soaking wet and wrapped in a towel."

She laughed. "Sure I do. Good night, Cruz."

He managed to maintain a smile until he walked out her door. As he retreated down the hotel corridor, he exhaled heavily. He decided he needed a cold shower, although he doubted anything but Gabriela herself would alleviate his rock-hard erection.

Cruz couldn't believe when he crossed the finish line and the checkered flag dropped, that he had actually won. That made two in a row. He'd thought Bakersfield was just a fluke, but not too surprising; after all, that was where he'd raced hundreds of times before in the entry-level southwest tour. But Vegas was a different story. Vegas was a super-speedway, and he'd beat it.

The guys were going nuts when he pulled into the pits after his victory lap.

"Where's Gabriela?" he asked after everyone congratulated him and noticed that the person he most wanted praise from wasn't around.

"Getting ready for the winner's circle," Flip said, grinning ear to ear. "That last lap, I knew you had it, just knew it."

Cruz felt like a winner when they placed him in the winner's circle, and cameras flashed all around him.

They all met in the garage, where NASCAR officials examined the car to make sure it met regulations. Gabriela and Flip spent about an hour in the garage with them. Cruz took the opportunity to shower and change.

"Okay, get the car ready and loaded into the trailer. We're leaving first thing in the morning," Gabriela said.

Cruz stood by the garage entrance and watched her. Miss organization, their fearless leader. He smiled. "What's your hurry?" he asked.

She whirled around. "Oh, Cruz, glad you're back. I've scheduled an interview with the local news. Let's go to the media room before they leave."

She practically led him by the hand.

"Slow down, Gabriela. Man, I've been sitting for a hundred laps, okay? My legs aren't ready to move at that speed."

"Sorry, I just don't want them to leave."

She was still dressed in her uniform, all covered up, but the breathless sound of her voice still made him think of her naked body in the shower. He'd suffered all night wanting her; he didn't need another sleepless night. He grabbed her hand and stopped her. *Tell her you want her. Kiss her. Do something.*

"What?" she asked.

He looked down at her, not able to summon the courage to act or speak.

She placed a hand on the side of his face. "Poor Cruz. Don't be nervous. I'll be right beside you. If you don't know how to answer a question, look at me, and I'll answer. Okay?"

God, Gabriela. Don't touch me. He nodded.

"Come on," she said with a smile. "I know you're in a hurry to take Flip out for his birthday."

Oh damn, that's right. He was going to ask her to go have a drink with him alone. Maybe he still could. "Do you want to come with us?" he asked. Then, after dinner, Flip would go gamble, and they would be left alone together.

"No, you should go alone. Besides, I'm going to turn in early tonight. Watch a movie and enjoy some peace and quiet."

He smiled. How could he argue with that? "I'll pick up the guitar early then, so I don't disturb you."

She opened the door to the media room. "Just knock on my door. I'll be waiting for you," she said. "Okay, here we go."

The news reporters were still there, and Cruz prepared himself for the interview, putting Gabriela's last statement out of his head. She'd be waiting for him . . . but not the way he wanted.

Gabriela left her speedway T-shirt in the media room—and this one she had to have. She'd showered and changed, and now exhaustion was hitting her like a ton of bricks. All she wanted was to crawl into bed, but retrieving the shirt would only take a minute. She opened the door to the media room and heard voices. Was Cruz still here? As she was about to peek around the corner, she heard her name and paused.

"I'm not saying she isn't doing a good job, but you could go so much further with an established team. Let's face it, she doesn't have the financial backing to take you all the way."

"This is my first season in the ARCA-Menards Series," Cruz's voice carried into the next room, quieter than the other man's. "I'm in no hurry."

"You should be. You need to consider your age and health and remember that you won't be the man you are today forever."

"I know."

"I can see you feel a certain amount of loyalty to her because of who her father was—."

"No," Cruz said curtly. "That's not it."

"Then consider my offer. I can make you a star, Cruz. She can't."

"You're probably right. I'll think about it and be in touch."

Gabriela felt as if she'd been punched in the chest. Who was Cruz talking to? Was he planning on leaving the team? She thought things were going well—that they were getting along. She didn't understand, but she'd heard enough. Stepping back, she looked at the door, wanting to leave before they realized she'd overheard.

She darted out of the media room and headed for her car. When she was halfway to the parking lot, she heard footsteps behind her.

"Hey," Cruz said, out of breath, jogging up beside her. "I got your T-shirt. You forgot it."

She stopped walking, took it, and stared at him. "Thanks."

He smiled. "Going back to the hotel?"

She nodded, but didn't start walking again.

"I'll go with you and get the guitar now. I'm meeting Flip in an hour in the lobby. I'll give it to him there."

"Fine."

He frowned. "Everything okay? Why are you looking at me like that?"

"Like what?"

He laughed nervously. "Like you don't recognize me. Never mind. Were you happy with the press conference? Went well, didn't it?"

"You were great, *a real star*." She forced herself to stop staring him down and continued walking to her car with Cruz following beside her. How could he smile and chat with her as he hadn't just been talking about her behind her back, plotting to leave her and all they'd worked so hard for?

When they reached her car, she stopped and searched his face. Should she ask? "Do you have anything you want to talk to me about?"

He looked a little taken aback, suddenly nervous. His smile had disappeared. "What do you mean?"

"Anything you want to tell me?"

"About . . .?"

"I don't know."

He shook his head. "I don't think so, Gabriela."

She lowered her gaze, disappointed. He *was* keeping something from her. She could tell from the look on his face. He couldn't even look her in the eye. "Let's go get the guitar," she said, wondering if he'd have the decency to tell her if and when he decided to find himself a new owner.

CHAPTER ELEVEN

Gabriela rushed to the pits of the California Speedway to wish Cruz luck before the race started.

When Cruz saw her, he got out of the car and pulled off his helmet. "Oh, so you decided to show up after all."

"I've been in the stands with possible new sponsors. What do you want?" They had the exceptional Terrace suites to watch the race from today. Since they were in California, many of their sponsors were attending, and she was taking the opportunity to show off the team. After winning both Bakersfield and Vegas, getting sponsors was getting easier—at least Cruz had a track record to show them now.

He reached out for her hand and examined her freshly painted nails. "I'm getting ready for a huge race, and you were thinking about your nails. That's just great."

She frowned at his odd behavior. Since Vegas, he'd been terse with her, as if her mere presence irritated him. She'd tried to put the conversation she'd overheard out of her mind. If he chose not to mention it, then she had to assume nothing was going on.

Maybe Cruz was nervous tonight. She closed her fingers around his gloved hand. “I should have been here a little before to make sure you had everything you needed. You’re right.”

“Hell, Gabriela. We have a race right here in California, and you miss the first two days.”

Was her attendance actually starting to mean something to him? All she’d missed were the qualifying run and pre-race activities. She wasn’t exactly needed daily anymore. Flip was in charge. Besides, she’d been feeling so drained the last few weeks, completely out of energy. “Is there a problem, Cruz?”

“You’re damn right there is. What’s the matter, Gabriela? Are you tired of playing race car owner? Are you back to worrying about fashion and getting your nails done?”

“What in the world are you talking about? Why would it bother you that I got my nails done?” She finally had some money to indulge just a little.

She let go of his hand, but he held on tight. His eyes were hard and critical, too much like they had been when they started working together. She couldn’t stand for things to go bad between them again, especially since she’d felt so close to him, not just a strong attraction, but a true friendship. “Cruz, come on. I don’t want to fight with you. What’s wrong? Tell me.”

He sighed, actually looked contrite. “You’re right. It’s just . . . I did good on the qualifying run, but something’s wrong with the car. It’s not rolling right.”

Now she was concerned. “Did you talk to the mechanics?”

“Yeah, they couldn’t find anything, but I know the car. Something’s wrong.”

She nodded. “I’ll pull the car from tonight’s race.” She let his hand go again, but he grabbed her arm and pulled her back.

“No way. Not this race.”

“I’m not taking any chances on you getting hurt.”

"Everything will be fine. After this race, we'll get it in for a thorough overhaul."

"And if you don't make it that far, then what?"

"Look, I just wanted you to be aware. I've talked to Flip, and he thinks it's okay. The mechanics say it's fine. It's just me." He shook his head. "I'm just nervous."

And he needed to talk to her? Did she soothe him? She chastised herself for being foolish. "I need you to feel comfortable, Cruz. We don't need any accidents."

He inhaled deeply, leaning his head back. "We won the last two races. You can't pull the car tonight."

"Pull the car?" Flip stepped beside them. "What the hell are you two talking about?"

"I told her something doesn't feel right and she—"

"Nothing's wrong with the car. Just take a breath and get inside."

"Flip, he's the driver, he knows the car—," Gabriela began.

"Damn it, *mujer*. Stop trying to hold his hand. You treat him like a child. Go back inside and watch the race. We're going to have win number three tonight."

"I'm not risking my driver." For the first time ever, she was annoyed with Flip.

"You both shut the hell up, and let's do this." Cruz put on his helmet. He swung his legs through the car window and settled into the seat. Danny belted him in.

Gabriela leaned inside his window as Danny moved back. She gripped Cruz's forearm. "I'll be in the stands. Any problem and have the guys come get me. Okay?"

He nodded and gave her the thumbs up.

"You're more important to me than this race," she said. "You know that, right?"

He stared at her for a second, then looked out the front windshield, effectively tuning her out.

He did twenty laps around the two-mile track with no problems, pulled in for a pit, then kept going. He lost one car position by the thirtieth lap. By the fortieth, he pulled in and the crew quickly pulled the hood open, did something to the engine, then closed it again. By the sixtieth lap, he slowed down so much it was evident there was a problem. He drove into the pits.

"What's he doing?" She said to herself.

"His engine blew," people around her started saying. "Too bad, he's been one of the top finishers."

Gabriela stood, one hand on her hip and the other tugging at a handful of hair. "His engine blew? How could that happen?"

Sheena, who attended the race since it was so close, stood as well. "Is he out of the race?"

"Yes, damn it!" She kicked a cup someone had left by her foot and sprayed the remaining contents around their feet.

"Hey, watch it, lady," someone called after her as she hurried down from the sunroof of the Terrace Suites.

She was so angry all she could think of was ringing Flip's and Cruz's necks. She stormed into the pits with Sheena on her heels.

Flip and the rest of the crew were making arrangements to pull the car into the garage—their faces long, shoulders stooped.

Flip pulled his baseball cap off and held it with both hands to his chest. "Shit, Gabby."

"I told you to keep the damn car off the track tonight."

"Engines blow all the time, Gabriela, you know that. It's part of racing."

"Next time, you listen to the driver. If he doesn't feel comfortable, we don't drive the car. Period."

"The mechanics couldn't find anything wrong."

"Then fire them and get new ones." Immediately, she felt guilty. She didn't really want to fire the mechanics. They were good workers. She was just frustrated. No wonder her father stayed in the lower divisions.

Flip lowered his eyes. "Shit, Gabriela. Shit." He turned away.

No one looked happy. Danny said, "We'll buy another engine. We'll get it switched over."

"It doesn't really help now, does it?"

"Nope. Sorry."

Gabriela frowned. "I'm out of here. Get the car back to our garage."

Danny nodded and reached for Sheena's arm.

"Not now," she said.

"I want to talk to you."

She raised an eyebrow. "I said, not now." Then she followed Gabriela out.

Gabriela knew she should have listened to her gut feeling. Cruz knew, damn him, but he let himself be influenced by the other men and the high of his previous wins.

She'd been excited also, so much so she could hardly breathe. But they didn't have to win every race or even attend them all. An engine was costly, and it wasn't worth risking damaging it. Now, after four races, they might have to pull out of the series.

Gabriela groaned when the knock on her door wouldn't stop. She dabbed at her stuffy nose with a tissue and forced her aching body out of bed. She pulled the front door open and saw Flip standing on the other side.

"Hi," he said.

"I'm sick."

"I've heard," he said. "Can I come in?"

She shrugged and then nodded. She sat on her couch, and he stood with his hands in his back pockets.

"You missed the last race."

"I've been sick." After months of stressing and struggling to stay afloat, her body wore out, and she caught the flu, which had lasted almost three weeks so far.

He nodded. "Cruz won Monterey."

"I know, he called me." And he'd talked more than ever, almost like he didn't want to hang up. He'd volunteered to do her grocery shopping, to bring her medicine, or to come by for company. She'd refused all his offers. She was in no mood to see anyone, especially Cruz.

"We have Irwindale in two weeks. You gonna be there?"

"I'll try."

He sat on the rickety coffee table, facing Gabriela, and she hoped it would hold his weight.

"It's been over a month since the California Speedway race. What's wrong, girl?"

"I've been—"

"Don't give me that sick thing again."

Well, she *had* been sick. But Flip was right; something else was bothering her. A depression had set in, and she didn't know why. She should be happy. Things couldn't be better. Her team was doing well. They had plenty of sponsors. Repairing the car drained their finances momentarily, even after the additional sponsors she'd signed on, but they were doing well.

Yet something was missing. Was it that she was finally mourning her father's death? Or was it that she had no one with whom to share her success? She didn't know, but she felt so alone.

Flip took her hand. "I made a mistake with Cruz that night. I wasn't thinking of him or the car, just winning. Big mistake for a crew chief."

She peered into his eyes. Every day since that race, she'd gone over it in her head. What if something worse had happened? What if it had been more than a blown engine? Would she be able to live with herself knowing she was the reason Cruz was on that track? "Until that night, I never gave it much thought that he could get hurt. All I wanted was to make money."

"You were the only one who told him not to race that day."

She looked down at their joined hands. "Every time he gets on that track, he risks his life."

Flip frowned. "He does it because he wants to."

She shook her head. "He does it because I asked him to; I bullied him into it."

Flip chuckled. "Girl, there's not a man who gets in a race car who doesn't want to be there."

"He wants to be an accountant; he told me so."

"If you think winning races and the thrill of driving that car isn't in his blood, you don't know Cruz."

"I know him."

Flip squeezed her hand. "I made a judgment error that night, and I scared you. I'm sorry. But you need to get well and come back, Gabriela. The team's not the same without you."

She smiled. "Right." As if she didn't know what they thought of her interference in 'their' team, what Cruz thought. Sure, he'd been nice lately, but he still resented her involvement.

"I mean it." He looked at her intently. "You started this. You made us all believe. Those boys know our team is a winner because you've told them so many times. They haven't seen you or heard from you, and they're starting to wonder."

She shook her head slowly. "What do I know? I'm just a spoiled rich girl with an art degree."

"You don't believe that. You got out there and pumped those guys up, got them to work. You showed up when we had no hope and, damn it, gave us some. We want it now, Gabriela. We *need* to win."

Gabriela wondered how much truth was wrapped in Flip's words. She thought winning the series was only important to her. Were they all as invested as Flip made it sound?

He let her hand go and stood. "Maybe it was the blind leading the blind, but you lead us just the same." He walked out of her apartment without another word.

If Flip didn't convince her, the visit she received three days later did. Cruz, Danny, Flip, and two maintenance workers, Chris and Eli, stormed into her apartment, a huge plant, four large pizzas, and two cases of beer as their offering.

"But—."

"No buts, we have nowhere else to go, and we're hungry," Flip said.

"His wife said we couldn't watch the game at his house," Cruz explained.

"Yeah, and my roommate has a girlfriend over, so my place is out," Danny said, making himself comfortable at her dining table.

The guys started passing beer bottles around. "Want one?" Flip asked.

"No."

Eli turned on her TV. "Man, this set is small."

She placed a hand on her hip and opened her mouth to tell them all to leave immediately when Chris bumped into her, kissed her cheek, and placed an arm around her shoulder. "Thanks, Gabriela, you're a real sport." He sat next to Eli.

"Mmm, have some pizza, Gabby," Danny said.

She watched them all make themselves comfortable and realized what they were doing. If she wouldn't come to them, they'd come to her. She tried not to smile at their sweet gesture.

"Feeling any better?" Flip asked.

"Yes, actually, I am," she said.

He handed her a beer bottle. "Drink, this will help cure you."

She took it and began tipping it when Cruz snatched it from her hand. "Actually, that's a bad idea. I bought you some ginger tea. My *abuela* always gave me ginger when I was sick."

He went into her kitchen and poured her a cup.

"Gee, thanks," she grumbled as she watched Cruz in her small kitchen, looking completely out of place.

He winked and nodded. "You should drink lots of ginger tea. Still having problems with your heater?"

"It works off and on."

"Let me take a look at it."

Cruz crouched down and opened the door at the bottom of the old wall heater. He lit the pilot a few times and watched it as he turned the knob. Then he stood. "Your thermocouple isn't working right."

"Thermo what?"

"It's the brain of the heater; tells the heater when to release gas, but yours isn't doing its job."

"Is that bad? I mean, is it hard to fix?"

The guys all cheered at something from the game on TV. Cruz glanced at them, then back at her. "I'll run to the hardware store for the replacement part."

"You don't have to do that, Cruz. Go watch the game with the guys. I'll let the apartment manager know it's broken."

"You've already done that, and it's still not working. I'll be right back."

Before she could argue, he left. She sat at the kitchen table. Flip came by and handed her a plate with two slices of pizza and her beer bottle back.

Gabriela laughed. She sat with her crew and ate pizza and drank ginger tea, and for the time being, felt better.

When Cruz came back, he lay on his back, took out a metallic piece of the heater, and installed a new one. He turned the heater on and tested it. A handsome smile graced his face as he rolled over and stood. "Tonight, you won't be cold."

"You gonna keep her warm," Eli said with a chuckle.

He received a smack on the head from Flip, an elbow in the ribs from Danny, and a dangerous stare from Cruz.

Gabriela smiled. "Thank you, Cruz." She held her hands up and felt the heat coming from the heater. "You're amazing. Is there anything you can't do?"

Cruz shrugged. "Let me clean up this mess." He went into the kitchen and found her broom. Gabriela took the old Thermocouple and threw it away. Cruz swept the baseboard and along the back of the couch. Then he got on his knees and disappeared.

Curious, Gabriela walked around the couch and saw him reading a white piece of crumpled paper. "What's that?"

He frowned and continued to read. She squatted beside him and realized what he was looking at. The letter from her father. She'd forgotten about it. It must have gotten stuck under the couch when she tossed it.

He turned and looked at her, a serious expression on his face, his eyes cold.

"I'll take that," she said, embarrassed that he had to read such a mean-spirited, critical letter—one that basically said how immature and incompetent her father thought she was.

He handed it to her without speaking. She debated whether to throw it away or save it and decided to place it in the box with her mother's mementos. She stood and went into her bedroom.

"Why didn't you sell the car like he suggested?" Cruz stood at the doorway of her bedroom. His arms crossed, his brows knit.

She took the box down and placed the crumpled letter inside. Then she sat on her bed and stared at Cruz, a lump in her throat. "To hell with him. That's why."

Cruz returned the stare, looked at the box, and then back at her. "Okay." He nodded. "To hell with him. So, get your ass back on the track where you belong."

"Is that where I belong?"

He uncrossed his arms and walked inside. He came within touching distance. "What do you think?"

She shrugged. "I heard you that night in Vegas, Cruz."

He frowned and looked confused.

"In the media room. I don't know who you were talking to, but I heard him telling you you could do better without me. On another team."

He continued to frown, but she could tell he now understood what she was talking about. "And you agree with him?"

"No, but—"

"Then do your job."

"I heard *you* tell him you felt no loyalty toward me."

He leaned down and placed a hand on her shoulder. "That's not what I said."

"I heard you."

"I told him that I wasn't leaving the team. He said it was because of my loyalty to your father, and *that's* what I said no to. Because the fact is, you're the reason I wouldn't leave the team. It has nothing to do with your father. I'm driving for and because of you."

He turned around, walking away from her.

"Cruz, wait."

"Get your rest, Gabriela. We have a season to win. And we can't do it without you."

She heard him turn off the TV and hustle the men out.

"Come on, Cruz. Wait 'til the game's over," Eli complained.

"Out. Gabriela's tired. Now."

They all called out their goodbyes, but Gabriela didn't move. She sat hugging the box, tears running down her face.

She had a family. She wasn't alone after all. And she loved them. All of them.

CHAPTER TWELVE

June

Cruz hung his duffle bag over his shoulder as he strolled out of the pits at Irwindale Speedway. He was exhausted tonight, but he took a moment to glance at the night sky. Now that the track lights were off, everyone was gone, and all was quiet, the stars twinkled in the sky as if to remind him that all the glitter and screams of the crowds were only momentary. At the end of the night, he was still Cruz, and he was still alone in this country.

Out of the corner of his eye, he saw someone high at the top of the bleachers. He turned his head and narrowed his eyes. Gabriela sat at the very top, leaning her back against the wall, all alone in the dark. She came after all and must have driven her own car.

He swallowed a lump in his throat. Apparently, he wasn't the only one dreading another night alone in a motel room. A cold, sterile bed was nothing to look forward to. He climbed the bleachers.

"It's late," he said when he reached the top, deciding not to make a big deal about her not letting them know she'd come.

She glanced at him. "Yeah."

Yeah, well, we should get the hell out of here, he wanted to say, but he sat beside her instead. "Good race tonight, huh?"

"You were impressive. A real celebrity. Did I see you signing autographs?"

Her voice was soft and wistful, and he wanted to pull her against him and hold her. For months, he'd been hard on her, pointed out every mistake, ridiculed her, told her to give up more times than he could count, yet here she was. She'd stuck it out, and now it really looked like they were making a go of this race team after all. Tonight, made win number four.

He angled his head and gave her a small smile. "You did. I can't believe kids want my autograph. I have you to thank for all this."

"Absolutely not. You've earned it yourself." She gazed at the empty track. "Is everyone gone?"

"Everyone except you and me."

She looked at him again. "You were on your way out. What stopped you?"

"A pretty girl sitting by herself in the dark."

"Don't stay on my account."

"Like I said before, it's late. You shouldn't be out here all alone." *And you should have been in pit row like the rest of the team.*

Gabriela laughed softly. "I don't need a bodyguard."

He nodded. "How about a friend?"

Again, she laughed and gazed down at her lap. "You and me? Friends? That would be the day. We don't like each other, remember?" Her tone was light, teasing.

He shrugged. "We like each other just fine. Why are you sitting here all alone, anyway?"

"Just thinking."

"About what?"

"Nothing. Everything."

Cruz reached for one of her hands. He held her icy fingers in his, feeling a curious protectiveness towards her. "For instance?"

She stared at their joined hands, resting on his knee. Although he wanted to see her eyes and figure out what she was thinking, she didn't look up.

She drew a deep breath. "For instance, I was wondering if my mom could see me from heaven, and if she could, what she was thinking about all this. Would she be proud of me, disappointed, worried? Would she want me hanging around all these men, who stink and curse and call me honey? If I had a little girl, I wouldn't want her out here."

Cruz frowned, pulled his hand away from hers as if he himself were one of the lowlifes tormenting her, and gazed at the track. "Me neither," he said.

She lifted her head, and he turned to look at her. Their eyes met. The one thing they shared was the desire to get out of the race scene as soon as possible. This wasn't the lifestyle of their dreams.

"I was also wondering if I should have a burger tonight, a bowl of soup, or skip dinner all together," she added. "See? Everything and nothing."

He smiled. "Skipping meals is never a good idea. How about we cross the street to Denny's, and you decide what you'd like to eat there?"

She shrugged. "Sounds good to me."

They stood and began climbing down the bleachers together. Their footsteps on metal sounded like pounding hammers in the quiet of the night.

"How long ago did your mom pass away?" Cruz asked, knowing that as long as he'd worked for her father, he'd been widowed.

"I was six years old."

A cold chill tickled the back of his neck. To lose a mother so young must have been hard. "Do you remember her?"

"Every detail. Her voice, the way she smelled, the songs she sang as she knitted, how she'd hold me . . . I remember everything about her."

Cruz wanted to put his arm around her so badly. He physically clenched his fist to resist the powerful urge. He'd always considered her to be privileged with everything Carlos Alende gave her, but tonight he felt like the one who had everything: two loving parents, a good home, a happy childhood, friends . . . . What did she have? Something Carlos was able to wipe away with a signature on a sheet of paper—money.

They walked across the empty parking lot, cleared of all cars but theirs. They crossed the quiet street together. It seemed not another soul in the world was awake. All the drivers and their fans had gone home. He held the door of the coffee shop open for her. She entered, and they were seated immediately. Only one other couple and an old man reading a magazine were in the restaurant.

At the table, he clasped his hands together and stared at her. "Well, I think she'd be proud of you. You're doing exactly what you said you would. You've gotten sponsors, and we're winning races . . . four out of six. We're on our way, Gabriela."

"You look happy about that."

He nodded. "I thrilled."

She lowered her eyes. "I'm glad."

He reached across and covered her hand, giving in to his need to touch her. "Thank you."

She looked at him. "For what?"

"For not giving up. For putting up with me. For making me a winner."

She shook her head. "I'm not making you a winner. You're doing that all on your own. You're remarkable."

No, she was the one who was remarkable. He wanted to leave this restaurant. To be somewhere private with Gabriela. He wanted to kiss her, make love to her. Unlike the fantasies of his youth, when they didn't know each other, this was a desire much deeper, much more real, and so strong he had to let go of her hand.

"Well, if our luck holds out, we'll be in the lead this year. Then you'll be in a perfect position to sell the team and move on to something else."

"Yeah," she said quietly, and poked the ice cubes in her water glass with her straw. "Most of our sponsors are already talking about supporting us for another year."

He caught her shy look, and wondered if she would consider staying with the team and seeing how far it could actually go. Of course, it didn't matter because *he* wasn't willing to do this any longer than he had to. He had a career waiting for him. Something clean and respectable. He didn't want to be a race car driver, he reminded himself. Not for her, not for anyone.

They ate in silence, except for a few casual sentences about the races they had won and what lay ahead.

"Can I ask you something about your friend, Sheena?"

Gabriela swallowed a bit of burger and nodded.

"Is she interested in Danny? Something is going on with them. He was upset because she told him she had a boyfriend. Do you know what's up?"

With a sigh, Gabriela put her burger down. "She has a fiancé."

"Wow."

"Yeah."

"So, she's not into Danny, I guess." He finished his food and pushed his plate aside.

"She likes him. They're sleeping together, but . . . Sheena is a little confused right now."

Cruz shook his head. "I'm kind of old fashioned. If a woman is engaged to one man, she shouldn't be sleeping with another."

Gabriela nodded. "Then I'm old fashioned too because I agree with you."

He smiled and reached for her hand, his strong fingers weaving between her delicate ones. "You are not anything like I thought you were. I'm sorry for everything I said to you in the past."

Squeezing his fingers and offering a wink. "Apology accepted."

As he walked her back to her car, his heart pounded. These new feelings for Gabriela frightened him. They were starting to go way past sexual desire. He cared about her. Every time he got on the track now, it was for her: to see her smile, to know he was the one responsible for her happiness. But tonight, her sadness seemed to go deeper, and he couldn't fix it by winning a race for her.

Flip had warned him something was wrong, that's why he'd organized the trip to her apartment with all the guys to cheer her up. That had backfired. After reading that letter from Carlos Alende, all he wanted to do was punch the bastard out and pull Gabriela into his arms. But Alende was dead, and Gabriela didn't need his pity. What did she need? He could see the pain in her eyes and felt helpless.

"Thank you for keeping me company tonight, Cruz," she said and unlocked her car.

He placed a hand on the hood. "Are you driving home tonight?" He was staying with the guys until tomorrow.

"I think so."

He moved closer. "I don't like you driving home alone, Gabby."

She eased a few strands of hair from her face and mouth and smiled sadly. "I don't either, but I'd rather sleep in my own bed tonight."

He pushed back the hair, which blew on her face again. He'd gladly sleep beside her. Would that make a difference? And if he kissed her just once, would she object? "I can go with you," he whispered, afraid to be rejected by her again.

Her eyes held a hint of tears before she moved closer and wrapped her arms around him.

He held her.

She clung to him, her head on his shoulder, her face buried in his neck. Soft lips and warm breath made him tighten his arms around her waist. His body reacted immediately, growing and hardening. He felt like a damn teenager. He didn't dare say a word, but lowered his head and inhaled her perfume, never wanting this moment to end. Unable to resist, he kissed her temple, and caressed her back, small circles leading down to her hips. She fit so perfectly in his arms, against his body. My God, did she feel good. He'd never wanted a woman as much as he wanted Gabriela at this moment.

She pulled back, a question in her eyes. Man, what was he doing? What was *she*?

Her eyes were dark as she stared into his. Then her gaze shifted to his lips, and she drew a shaky breath. Damn it, she wasn't going to do this to him. He'd promised to keep his hands to himself, and he wasn't going to be the one to break the deal. As much as he hated to do it, he released his hold.

She ran the side of her face against his and kissed his cheek. "Thank you. I really needed that hug."

He chuckled. "You're such a tease, Gabby."

She looked shocked, hurt. "Tease?"

"Don't pretend you don't know what I'm saying."

She searched his face, frowned, and nodded. "I know, Cruz."

Of course, she knew. If she said she hadn't felt his erection in his jeans, she'd be a liar. He wanted her with every cell of his body, and he deserved the gold medal of honor for his restraint. "And you want me to tell you something *I* know."

She gazed at him. "Okay."

He ran his knuckles down the side of her neck and across her shoulder blade, stopping provocatively between her breasts, extending his fingers. "I know if I touched you the right way, said the right things . . . ." He gripped her chin, not worried about being gentle. He wanted to see her eyes. "I know I could have you."

She cocked an eyebrow, and he waited for her to deny the attraction between them that was so glaringly apparent to him. "Well, what's stopping you?" she asked.

He let her go and clamped his jaw tight, not sure if that was an invitation, a challenge, or a simple question. He took her upper arms and moved in close, their lips almost touching. He startled her because she inhaled sharply and stared at him.

Kiss me. Kiss me once, Gabriela, and nothing will stop me. She had to initiate that kind of intimacy. He wouldn't be accused of disrespecting their precious relationship again.

But she didn't make a move.

He closed his eyes. "You." He sighed. "You're stopping me."

"I don't have the strength to stop you. I don't want to."

He opened his eyes and looked at her. He didn't want her to submit because she was tired or lonely. He wanted her to be enthusiastic and as engaged as he was. Loneliness was the worst reason of all to end up in someone's bed. "Yeah, well, somewhere along the line, you've become more important to me than a quicky in a motel room. I can't play the seduction game with you, Gabby. Making love to you . . ." He shook his head. "Let's just say it would be for real if it happened."

"Wow," she said, easing out of his arms, looking alive for the first time tonight and maybe a little frightened. "If that's true . . . maybe we have become friends after all."

He smiled and nodded. They'd become friends. No doubt about that. In fact, he was afraid he was falling in love with Gabriela.

CHAPTER THIRTEEN

July

Although it wasn't a race week for him, for publicity purposes, Cruz parked his car at the entrance of the Bakeracetrackce track and spoke with fans as they entered. Everyone at this 'home' track loved that he led the ARCA-Menard West with his most recent win in Portland. One of their own was making it in NASCAR.

Last April, when Cruz had displayed the car, they'd helped raise a few hundred dollars for charity, so both Cruz and Gabriela were eager to do it again. Like before, Cruz made a deal with the track to use one side of his car for fan signatures, only for tonight. People paid to sign their name on his car, and at the end of the night, all the money would be donated to charity.

Gabriela collected more business cards. Sponsors weren't exactly knocking on her door, but businesses were more than willing to listen to her pitch. Over a shared box of pizza one night, she'd confided that they were making more money than she'd hoped, but he'd already realized that from the size of his paychecks every month. By the end of the season, she'd actually be able to sell this team at a huge profit. For that, he was glad. If making money and getting out of this business made her happy, he was going to make sure she got what she wanted.

"The tires don't have grooves because we need them to heat up on the track. That allows for more speed." Cruz pointed to the tire. He crouched beside the car with three little boys who were listening with interest.

He turned his head as Gabriela walked to the car and stood beside him. His eyes traveled up her long, sexy legs and easy curves of her body until he finally reached her face. He was glad they'd admitted how attracted they were to each other. Some of the tension between them eased, and they actually seemed to be more comfortable together.

He stood and looked over her shoulder at the man she'd been trying to convince to invest in a partial sponsorship until the end of the season. "You've been talking to that guy for half an hour. Did he ask you out on a date?"

Gabriela slipped off her sunglasses and searched Cruz's eyes. His question surprised her. Was he teasing her? "No." She laughed. "But he did offer me money."

He smiled. "Fool. He should have tried for a date first."

The little boys he had been talking to were desperately trying to get his attention. She looked at the kids. "You've got the cutest fans."

He nodded, looking proud to have the attention of eager kids who were in awe of what he did. "Cute fans, a gorgeous owner. What more can a guy ask for?"

His attractive smile and flattering words brought a twinkle of pleasure inside. Lately, he seemed satisfied with everything, and his attitude toward her had thoroughly changed. Especially since that late-night dinner they'd shared at the coffee shop a couple of weeks ago . . . and that dangerous hug in the parking lot. They both could have easily succumbed to loneliness, given in to their mutual desires, but they hadn't. Their relationship was stronger for it. She felt a deep, vital connection with Cruz, a warm feeling that drew her to him more than ever.

"We need to go to the announcer's booth for a little interview. Want to leave your fans for a few minutes?"

"You bet."

They climbed the stands, and for an instant, Gabriela thought about how good they looked together. About the same height, he was strong, handsome, sexy, and next to him, she felt beautiful and feminine. She wondered if it was only wishful thinking on her part or if others saw them that way too. The sexy driver, and as he put it, his gorgeous owner. She shook her head and laughed. She'd read too many fairy tales.

"What's so funny?" he asked.

"What? Oh, nothing."

As they entered the announcer's booth, they were given headphones and placed on either side of Billie. Billie announced the end of the first race, then turned off her mike. "I'll talk up the charity signing, then ask you a few questions about your team, plug your sponsors, stuff like that. Sound good?"

"Sure," Gabriela said.

Cruz leaned back in his chair and gave her a thumbs up.

"You look terrific, Gabriela. How have you been?" Billie adjusted her headset.

"Very busy." She pointed at Cruz. "Following a star around is exhausting." Cruz watched them stone-faced with hooded eyes. The attention should be on him, and she didn't want Billie to overlook him.

Billie smiled at Cruz. "And a star he is. Of course, I've known that from the first day he walked on this track."

Cruz didn't offer a word. Gabriela studied him, wondering if Billie and Cruz had ever had more than a friendly relationship.

Billie punched a button and began talking. "I'm here with the Alende race team, owner, Gabriela Alende, and driver Cruz Ortega. They're here today letting ya'll get a peek at their winning car, and for a few bucks you can sign your name on the side tonight. They're raising money for what, Gabriela?"

"It's going to child welfare. All the information is in the booth beside the car, and volunteers from the organization are there also to answer any questions."

She asked Cruz a few questions about his last wins, and Cruz responded with quick staccato answers.

"What's it like working for a woman?" Billie asked.

Cruz laughed. "Ms. Alende is a professional, dedicated owner who has taken this team and polished it with her own special style."

"I remember the first day I introduced you two. You didn't seem so pleased that day."

He met Gabriela's eyes. "That was a long time ago, Billie."

"And you certainly seem to be working well together now. What are the plans for next season? Will you enter the Xfinity series?"

Gabriela leaned toward the mike. "We're taking one season at a time. We're thrilled with our success this season. We've all worked hard, and we're enjoying that right now."

"I guess we'll just have to wait and see, then. We'll certainly keep an eye on your team. Ya'll can meet and talk to Gabriela and Cruz by the front entrance."

Billie clicked off the mike as the next race was about to start. "Thanks guys."

Gabriela stood. "That was fun."."

"You can stay for a while if you want, Cruz," Billie offered. "I don't get to talk to you anymore now that you're traveling all over the western U.S."

"I'm going back to the car."

"Those little boys are probably still waiting by your car. Kids just love him," Gabriela said to Billie.

"It's my car they love."

Billie shrugged. "And your female fans? Are they as impressed by your equipment?"

Cruz left without comment.

Gabriela's eyes narrowed, and she tilted her head slightly as she gazed at Billie, who was turning on her mike and adjusting her headphones.

The warm breeze felt good as they stepped outside. "Ah, this is beach weather," Gabriela said. "I miss it soooo much."

He took her arm and pulled her to the top bench, where they could see the entire track. "Tell me about it." Cruz had a relaxed, approachable look now that the interview was over.

"What? The beach?" What she really wanted to talk about was Billie. They sat beside each other. "What did Billie mean with all those suggestive comments?"

"Tell me about the beach."

"Tell me about Billie."

He groaned, gazing out into the distance. "Youthful, stupid mistake."

Why did it hurt to know they'd shared any kind of intimacy together? "Mistake?"

"I was young, alone, thought she cared. She didn't."

Gabriela was surprised. Was he saying Billie had used him and not the other way around? "You sound like *you* still care."

He shook his head, staring down at his fingernails. "I felt like a fool when I found out she had a reputation for seducing new, young drivers."

"Poor baby," Gabriela said.

A laugh escaped his lips. "You came on to me in your dad's office first, then her. I got a big head and quite an ego."

Now, *she* groaned. Was he ever going to let her forget that kiss? "I was an innocent child."

He shook his head again, pinning her with a knowing look. "You were a sexy teenager, only a few years younger than me."

"True. Okay, I was shameful, I admit it."

He smiled. "Anyway, I thought I was quite a stud before I caught Billie making out with another driver beside her car and realized I didn't mean anything to her. And before you ignored me each time you came to see your dad."

"You're still quite a stud."

"Naw. I'm over that ego stuff now."

She laughed. "Oh yeah, since when?"

"Since I made a tasteless pass at my boss on her desk. I still cringe when I remember the look on your face."

Gabriela continued to laugh. "You mean I'm the one who compelled you to reform?"

"It's the truth," Cruz said, his voice suddenly low and sincere. "You helped me remember who I am."

Her laughter subsided at his sudden seriousness. They'd come a long way from her childhood kiss to his attack on her desk to their heartwarming hug in the parking lot. She was glad they could sit together and laugh about it all—well, almost all of it.

"Anyhow." He clapped his hands together as if to say he was finished talking about that. " Billie is Billie, a big flirt, but she's a nice lady. Maybe like your friend, Sheena."

"Sheena doesn't flirt with every guy. By the way, she told me that she and Danny had a big fight when he found out she's engaged to Griffin."

"What did she expect?"

"I think she was okay with the two of them using each other for sex and lighthearted fun. She didn't think Danny wanted anything more, even though I warned her."

"No wonder he was acting like a kicked dog the other day. We all learn eventually that women can't be trusted."

"Hey," she shoved his shoulder with her own.

"Okay, some women." He held his hands up defensively. "Billie was my reality check. I guess Sheena is his."

"Cruz, you are such a chauvinist," she said, teasing him. "Still curious about the beach?"

"Sure."

"Haven't you been?"

"A couple of times. I didn't get to go to college in Santa Barbara like you did, though. You probably lived on the beach."

"I was there a lot. Made studying difficult."

"Your father used to get so angry when he'd call and hear your place packed with people. He was sure you were up to no good, ruining your life, getting no studying done."

"He was right about some of it." She didn't want to talk about her father, especially not with Cruz. She wondered why her father had confided in him about her. All that should have been personal between father and daughter.

"What was he right about?"

"I had a good time in Santa Barbara." She shrugged, refusing to discuss her behavior or her father's accusations. "I wish you could have spent some time there with me and my friends. You would have liked it."

He angled his head and met her gaze, his eyes full of something she didn't dare to name, perhaps lament, perhaps distance. "I'm not part of your crowd, Gabriela."

She stared closely at his handsome face. "I never had a crowd." She waited for him to show the disbelief her father always had—to call her a liar. He didn't.

"You know what I mean. I haven't had the luxury of *enjoying* college. I've had to go between jobs."

"That's because you're too serious. All you think of is work. You need some fun in your life."

"I have fun."

"Yeah, right. When this season is over, I'm going to take you to the beach, and we're going to sit under the sun and do nothing for hours. No studying. No making money."

"You call that fun, huh?"

"Yes, fun and relaxation."

"That sounds like an invitation I'd be a fool to pass up." He eyed her interest, a glint sparkling in his eyes. "I assume you'll wear a bikini?"

With a smile, she shook her head. "Your attention will be absorbed by the feel of the warm sun on your skin, the peaceful, repetitive sound of the waves. You'll probably fall asleep and won't even know I'm there."

He burst into laughter. "Yeah, right. You tell yourself that."

"The point is that you have to take time to enjoy your life. For me, it was spending hours at the beach, at museums, making art."

"That's fine for you, but I don't like to waste time on frivolous things. I'm basically a simple man, Gabriela. I want a good job, a nice house, a wife, about four kids, and that's it."

"Four kids?" She was unable to close her mouth.

"Good number, don't you think?" He leaned into her and bumped her shoulder playfully like she'd done to him.

"If you can find a woman who will want to stay home and do nothing but take care of kids."

"And take care of me." He smiled mischievously. "Especially in bed."

"You really are a dinosaur."

He placed an arm around her shoulder and pulled her close to his body, a move so unexpected, she stiffened. "Someday, I'm going to take you to Mexico, to meet my parents. Then you'll see what marriage is really about."

She frowned and gazed up at him. "What's it about?"

He stared at her for a few disquieting moments. Then he smiled and looked up at the sky, a distant look in his eyes. "It's about love, sharing, fidelity . . . it's about sacrifice and pain sometimes too."

She smiled as she watched Cruz. This was a side of him she'd never seen. A side she liked very much.

"It's hard to explain, but when you see two people who deeply love each other live together, it fills you with a warm, hopeful feeling about life."

She'd never seen people who were really in love. Maybe Sheena's parents or Rob and Jolie. But she wasn't around them long enough to witness small kisses or secret looks or small caresses, things she figured married people who were in love shared. "What are your parents like?"

"My dad is strong, a provider. All he's done is work his whole life."

She nodded. "Sounds like someone I know."

He looked at her tenderly. "I'm proud to be like him. He's taught me a lot." His voice deepened, and he winked. "To be a real *macho*."

She watched him, a warm feeling growing in her heart. Cruz had learned well. Masculinity seeped out of him in the way he walked, stood, moved—the way he made a woman feel when he held her in his arms. But she didn't want to think about that. "And your mother?" she asked.

"My mom has always stood beside my father. Her job was to care for us. Keep us clean, fed, and healthy. If I found a woman like my mother, I'd marry her tomorrow."

She pulled away and shook her head. "Times have changed, Cruz. Haven't you noticed?"

He rested his back against the wall. "I've noticed."

She stood and offered her hand to help pull him up.

He took it, stood, held it for a few moments, then let it go and smiled. "Think I'll find her?"

She took a few moments to think before she answered. How many women would be happy to bear this man's children and wait for him to come home to her every night—to her bed? Probably anyone lucky enough to have those warm brown eyes look lovingly at her. "Well, if not, you can always hire a housekeeper and a cook."

"Very funny." He narrowed his eyes and tipped her chin with his hand. "How about you let this dinosaur buy you a drink after we leave here?"

Gabriela's heart stopped. She loved his touch. More and more, she wanted him to touch her all over—with his hands, mouth, body. She'd been on the verge of asking him to do just that when he held her a couple of weeks ago. She was attracted to him, extremely so. But attraction was nothing but a physical appreciation. Something she could ignore. And she had to.

"I'd rather make that dinner." A drink sounded too intimate. What would they do afterward when they were feeling warm and relaxed and not thinking quite clearly?

He shrugged. "Dinner, it is."

CHAPTER FOURTEEN

August

Gabriela flipped burgers on the barbeque while Sheena made a salad. Griffin was coming over and they were going to have dinner with her parents before Gabriela left for the race in Washington with the team in the morning.

"You should have invited Cruz over," Sheena said, standing at the work-table under the pergola covered with colorful hanging planters of white and yellow Honeysuckles and beautiful Fuschias that attracted humming-birds.

"Why would I invite him to your family's house?"

She tossed cherry tomatoes into the salad and eyed her slyly, angling her head. "Aren't you two a couple now?"

"No." Gabriela didn't want anyone to get that idea, especially Sheena.

"Could have fooled me and everyone else, too. Danny, back when he was talking to me, said Cruz is completely into you."

Gabriela picked up a tray and began transferring the burgers. "Anyone want cheese?"

"No," Sheena said. "Don't you like him?"

"Of course, I like him. He's my driver. That's it." She glanced up, relieved to see Griffen stroll out onto the back patio.

"You finally made it," Sheena said. "Gabriela just took the burgers off the grill."

"I rushed over from the university. And I can only stay for a couple of hours." He leaned across and gave Gabriela a peck on the cheek and went to wrap his arms around Sheena.

But she eased back. "What the fuck, Griffin. You're not staying the night?"

"No, I'm headed to the desert for a shoot. I'm interviewing—"

"You have to be fucking kidding me."

He held his arms up rather than wrapping them around her. "Didn't I tell you?"

"Apparently not, and you didn't invite me to go with you either."

He ran a hand through his untrimmed, dirty-blond hair. "I've been preoccupied. There's nothing for you to do while I'm working anyway."

She slammed a pair of tongs on the table. "You're always working. Maybe I should go with Gabriela on the road. At least *those* men pay attention to me."

"What the hell does that mean?" Griffin shouted.

Gabriela wasn't sure if she should slip out or try to lighten the mood.

Sheena placed a hand on her hip. "It means I seriously have more fun with Danny than I do with you these days."

"Danny? The kid you were playing video games with?"

"He's not a kid, and . . . never mind."

Griffin turned away. "If what you want is a teenage mechanic, by all means, let me know."

Gabriela picked up the tray of hamburgers. Yep, it was time for her to discretely disappear into the house.

"You arrogant, condescending, elitist piece of shit," Sheena shouted. While Griffin shouted over her, calling her an overindulged brat who didn't understand anything about work and following a dream.

Gabriela leaned on the kitchen counter and sighed. This was bad. As she was trying to decide what to do with the burger patties, Sheena's parents came home, and Griffin stormed through the kitchen and out of the house, slamming the front door on his way out.

"What happened?" Sheena's mother asked, her eyes wide and her face frozen in confusion.

"Just a little disagreement," Gabriela said. "I'll go check on Sheena."

Sheena sat on a rattan chair, holding her head.

"Hey," Gabriela said. "Are you okay?"

"I don't know," she whispered. "I told him the thought of marrying him made me want to get into your racecar and slam it into a wall."

"Oh, wow. That's horrible. Is that how you really feel?"

"No, I want to put him in the car and have him slam into the wall. Why would I kill myself when I just want *him* gone?"

Gabriela sat across from her. "Well, you got what you wanted. He's gone. What did he say?"

"That I was pathetic, a dance and music major who was never going to amount to anything, and that I didn't have to run a car into any walls because he was calling off the marriage. 'You're free,' he said."

"He didn't mean it. He loves you. Give him a little time to cool off, and —."

"There was no marriage to call off. Neither one of us has planned anything. He proposed so long ago that I don't even remember why we wanted to get married anymore. It's over."

"I'm sorry."

"Don't tell my parents. I'll break it to them."

"They heard you two shouting and saw Griffin storm out of the house."

"Shit."

"Look, I'll leave you alone to talk to them. I've got to get home to pack."

"You haven't even eaten yet."

"I'll make my burger to go."

"I'm sorry that I ruined the night, Gabriela. I was just so tired of him fitting me into his schedule as if I'm an irritation that's in the way of his precious films."

Gabriela stood and bent down in front of Sheena's chair. "Don't apologize. I know you haven't been happy with him. That you've been disappointed."

"I was hoping he'd remember how much he loved and wanted me, but I'm tired of waiting."

Gabriela hugged her. "I wish I didn't have to leave tomorrow."

Sheena gave her a soft smile. "You go. Be with your race car driver that you aren't at all interested in."

Gabriela shook her head and smiled back. "You're terrible, but I love you. And I'm sorry things didn't work out with Griffin."

She shrugged. "Me too."

With Flip's direction, the mechanics loaded the car onto the trailer. "We've got two more guys coming this time," Flip said.

"How are we going to get them all to Washington?"

"Put them in the coach. I'll go with Gabriela in her car."

She flashed him a quick look. He was going to ride with her all the way to Monroe?

"That okay, Gabriela? I can drive."

She shrugged. "Should you be driving? You need to rest before the race."

"I'll be fine."

Riding for so many hours alone with Cruz would be nerve-racking. He no longer hid the look of interest, of male appreciation. And it bothered her because her body reacted to it so strongly. And the extra attention wasn't like the rude come-on he'd attempted in her office. This was different; this was subtle, yet way more effective.

She set aside her childish worries and continued to check and double-check her list to ensure they had everything they needed in the trailer.

As soon as they got on the road, she rolled down the window and began to relax. She no longer rode in the coach with the men but followed in her car. She found that she enjoyed the quiet time alone to think. But it did get lonely sometimes, so maybe it would be nice to drive with someone else for a change, to sit back and enjoy the scenery. Cruz turned on the radio, tuning it to a jazzy station. She liked his taste in music. For the first eight hours, they drove with little interaction and stopped only once to eat and use the restrooms. When they reached San Francisco, he stopped for the night at a motel.

Gabriela needed some exercise after so many hours of sitting. "I saw a park a few blocks back," she said as Cruz pulled their overnight bags out of the trunk. "I'm going to change and go for a jog."

"Great idea. That's exactly what I need. Mind if I tag along?"

In a way, she did. She'd spent all day with Cruz and could use some time alone. But she shook her head. "I'll meet you by the car in about fifteen minutes."

He winked, handed her a key, and disappeared into his motel room. She slipped into the room adjacent to his and changed into running gear.

When Gabriela walked back out, she saw Cruz leaning on her Kia, waiting for her. Was it a surprise that he looked annoyingly sexy in running shorts and a tight black sports T-shirt? She'd watched him many times do pull-ups, push-ups, sit-ups in the garage. Cruz had an enormous amount of upper body strength without having excessive bulk. Danny had explained how necessary it was for a driver to be physically fit to withstand the hours spent in a car. None of that had interested her. What had totally absorbed her attention had been the beauty of Cruz's body in motion. And she fantasized about that body lying above hers.

Now, without even moving, the sight of his muscular back held her in rapt attention.

Cruz glanced over his shoulder. "There you are." He smiled. "Ready?"

"Yeah."

They walked to the park to warm up. Then when they got there, they began jogging at a steady pace. The park probably had a circumference of a half mile. On the sixth lap, Gabriela stopped. Three miles was more than enough. She felt good; her body needed the physical exertion to get her blood pumping and exhaust her muscles before bed.

"That's it?" Cruz asked. He breathed rapidly, perspiring heavily.

She wiped her own brow. "Yes, but don't let me stop you. Keep going."

Cruz laughed and bent at the waist, stretching the back of his calves. "Are you kidding? I'm dying. I kept praying you'd stop soon."

She smiled. "Liar. I know you run more than this." She couldn't help but stare at his well-sculpted, iron-like legs, wondering what those black hairs would feel like against her skin.

He placed his hands on his hips. "Oh yeah? And how do you know that?

"Danny told me."

"Danny told you how much I run?"

"Five miles. Every day."

They walked back to the Motel 7. "Interesting topic of conversation."

She glanced at him from the corner of her eyes. "Not at all. We talk about you a lot."

"Really." No question, just a statement. "Why?"

Because she was interested in everything about him. She already knew so many personal things—the clean, soapy smell of him first thing in the morning, how much cream he put in his coffee, how he called his parents every Sunday at the same time. Maybe she had no business knowing these things, but from spending so much time with him, she'd learned.

They reached the motel and stopped at her door.

"If you don't answer, I'll assume the worst," he said

"What's that?"

"That you're infatuated and can't get enough of me." He smiled, obviously teasing her.

"I'm way past the infatuation stage," she said, teasing him back. But was it true? Was she developing romantic feelings for Cruz that could get her into big trouble?

"Oh yeah? Why don't we go to my room? You can find out a few more things about me."

She raised her eyebrows in question, surprised he'd suggest such a thing. They'd fallen into easy flirting lately, but nothing as direct as that.

He chuckled. "I meant to watch a movie. You don't know my taste in movies yet, do you?"

"No, I don't, and I think I'll pass."

"You sure? It's still early."

"I'm sure. There'll be no late-night movie watching tonight."

He leaned in and dropped a kiss on her cheek. "Sleep tight then. If you change your mind, you know where to find me."

"Sleep well, Cruz."

He eased back, but before he opened his door, he gazed at her. "You sleep well, too. And Gabriela?"

"Yeah?"

"You have a pair of very sexy legs. When we go to the beach, you definitely need to wear that bikini." He winked and disappeared behind his motel room door.

The next morning they drove again for long hours, stopping in Eureka only to rest and stretch their legs, but ended up spending most of the afternoon walking and talking, mostly about his childhood and his parents. Gabriela listened with a bit of envy. How she wished she'd grown up with two loving parents.

When they got back on the road, they realized the stop ended up being costly. By the time they got to Oregon, they encountered a full-fledged storm, and the rain slowed them considerably. Cruz had to reduce his speed but continued to forge ahead, wiping the fogged windows constantly. Finally, he cursed and pulled to the side of the road.

"What's wrong?" Gabriela stretched in her seat.

"I can't see a damn thing."

"Well, what are you going to do?"

"Nothing. Sit here."

"But the storm is supposed to last for a couple of days."

"When it eases up, we'll go. For now, I'm going to sit tight, maybe take a nap, and wait."

He eased his seat back, and Gabriela watched him, not believing that he was serious. They couldn't just sit here on the side of the road. He leaned across her.

"What are you do--? Aahh," she screamed as her backrest dropped.

"Take a nap," Cruz said, braced just above her

She met his eyes and swallowed. To be on her back with Cruz's hard body stretched across her exactly where she'd dreamed of having him for so long made her pulse pick up speed. "I don't think I can," she said.

He glanced at her lips, then back into her eyes, before he pushed away from her. "Try." He lay back in his own seat and closed his eyes.

Gabriela watched him and, a few minutes later, noticed his breathing had actually gotten deeper. She turned her head and stared at the car roof, sighing. She wasn't tired, but Cruz must be if he could fall asleep that quickly. Closing her eyes, she tried to sleep.

A couple of hours later, she heard him awaken and turn on his side. "You're not sleeping."

"No," she was daydreaming, listening to the beating of the rain on the car, watching the lightning crack in the sky.

He smiled, his face still sleepy. "What have you been doing?"

"Just enjoying the rain."

He nodded, then turned onto his back and stretched, a deep, rumbling moan escaping from inside his throat. "Hasn't let up, huh?"

Gabriela could not take her eyes off him. His arm and chest muscles tightened and contracted as he extended his body in the small car. His belly barely dipped from the number of corded muscles that transversed across it. His legs were also solid muscle from driving.

He turned his head. "Gabriela?"

"Yes, it's still raining." She said quickly and looked away. "Don't you hear it?"

He placed his hands behind his head. And smiled. "You know, in Mexico, as a young boy, I remember these wild storms. My cousin and I would go outside and try to jump over puddles as the rain pelted us. Of course, we'd end up with mud all over our pants and shoes, then track it inside on my grandmother's clean floor." He chuckled. "Boy, did she get angry."

Gabriela turned to her side, propping her head on an arm, and stared at Cruz. He looked so different lately—almost boyish. "What did she do to you?" Gabriela asked.

Cruz grinned. "She'd grab her broom and chase us back outside, make us take our shoes, pants, and shirt off on the porch, then wrap us with these large, soft towels that swallowed us up. She'd make us sit on the sofa while she made us hot chocolate." Cruz rolled back on his side, facing her. "The whole time, she'd complain about all the extra work we'd just given her and tell us how lucky we were that our parents were not there. She'd warn us that if we didn't behave the rest of the night, she'd tell them, and we'd live to regret it. Of course, she never had any intention of saying a word to our parents."

"She sounds like a beautiful, loving soul."

He nodded. "Grandparents are the best, aren't they?"

"I don't remember much about mine. My grandparents lived in Mexico too, but after my mother died, my father never returned."

"Why?"

She gazed over Cruz's shoulder out of the window behind him, which was completely fogged over now. "He didn't take my mother's death well. I think the way he dealt with it was to block everything out except his work."

Cruz stared at her silently, making her uncomfortable. Finally, she met his eyes.

"Even you?" he asked.

She rolled onto her back again. "Should you try driving again?"

He reached across and touched her shoulder. "No, I want you to answer my question."

"What does it matter, Cruz?"

"Because I want to know."

"I told you, he changed. You thought he was a loving father, but he wasn't. Maybe he wanted to be and didn't know how."

Cruz inched closer. "Is that what you think?"

"No," she faced him. "I think I reminded him of my mother, and he didn't want to have anything to do with me." There, she'd put it into words, the rejection she'd always felt.

Cruz moved his hand to her neck, his thumb caressing her jawline. "I thought it was you that—"

"I know."

He pulled himself up on his elbow and slid as far over as the middle console would allow. Then he gripped her chin and turned her face. His lips touched hers ever so softly, tentatively. A soft, feather-light whisper of a kiss that sent a shiver through her whole body.

He pulled back. "Damn it, Gabby, it's getting harder and harder not to touch you."

She drew in a breath, finding this natural act difficult with the sudden lack of oxygen in the car. She wanted him to touch her, no longer caring why he shouldn't, no longer remembering her own objections.

He continued, "Since you first kissed me seven years ago, I've been crazy about you. I can't ignore it anymore."

Gabriela placed her hands on his shoulders. She didn't know what to say. "Why didn't you ever tell me? I mean, before we got involved in racing together. Why did you wait seven years?"

"At first, you were a child. I thought I was crazy. Then, every time I saw you with your father, you were so full of yourself in your fancy clothes and superior, elitist attitude, I didn't think you'd waste your time on a guy like me. After a while, I honestly didn't like you."

She allowed herself the pleasure of running her fingers along his face, rubbing the forehead, usually covered with creases. Little did he know it wouldn't have been her to object but her father, the man who Cruz thought was so wonderful. "What do you think now?"

His breathing deepened, and he stared at her with passion-filled eyes. "Now, I'm in awe of you. I'm constantly impressed with what you've accomplished. I respect and adore you. Now, I know you're kind and generous, and I want you." He captured her hand. "And I know you want me, too."

"I'm attracted to you; I won't deny that."

He ran his fingers between her own. "Yes, but that's not the same as wanting *me*, is it?"

"I guess I don't know what you mean."

"You're always so sad, Gabby. Alone and distant. There's a part of you I can't reach, and you're not willing to let me get closer. There's this chemistry between us for sure, but maybe you want me because we spend so much time together, and you need me to help you out of your financial crunch. So, you're grateful, you're—."

"Wow." She laughed bitterly. "What a pitiful picture you're painting. A poor, lonely, needy woman clinging to the only warm body who notices her."

"That's not what I said."

"What are you saying then?" The sharpness of her tone brought back how they used to talk to each other, and she wanted to rein in her temper, but did he realize how condescending he was?

His tone changed, too, as did the softness in his eyes and the relaxed muscles in his face and jaw. "That under different circumstances, if you weren't in financial need, you wouldn't have any interest in me."

What a hurtful, insulting thing to say. She pulled her hand free of his and put pressure on his shoulders to move him away, then sat straight in the sticky vinyl seat. "If I weren't in financial need? I'm not! I have made us all a hell of a lot of money, in case you haven't noticed."

"You know what I mean. If your father hadn't died and we hadn't been pushed together, you wouldn't have given me a second glance."

She shook her head in disappointment. "You still give me so little credit. I'm still nothing but a stuck-up rich girl to you, aren't I?"

"Come on, Gabriela. Don't twist my words. You know what I'm saying."

"If my father hadn't died and left me that car, I wouldn't have had any reason to return to the track and for us to work together. Obviously. But, let me tell you something, Cruz. I've never cared what you wore, what kind of work you did, or how much money was in your bank account. I've never judged you. But you've been doing that to me since the first day we met."

"I said I was wrong. I apologized, and—."

"When? I must have missed it."

Cruz's scowl appeared. He lifted his backrest. Then he took a rag he'd been using earlier and began wiping the windows.

She crossed her arms and stared straight ahead. Was he just going to drive again in the middle of their argument? Now that he'd admitted how long he'd wanted her, now that he'd insulted her? No, he wasn't. She reached across and pushed the start button to turn the car off.

"What the hell are—?"

"Why do men think if they shut something out, it'll go away?"

He pushed the button again to turn the car on.

She rolled down the window and threw her keys outside and then turned the car off.

He slammed his open hand on the steering wheel. "What did you do that for?"

"Because we're not finished. I'm sick and tired of your insulting insinuations that I ever treated you differently because you weren't wealthy or that I thought you weren't good enough for me. I never have."

"I know that!"

"Then stop treating me like I'm someone I'm not. I can't stand it anymore." Tears pooled in Gabriela's eyes from anger and frustration. Damn it, she didn't want to cry. She pushed open her door and walked out into the rain on the side of the forested highway.

Cruz ran out after her. "Gabby, are you crazy? Come back in the car."

"I've never deserved the way you've treated me." The emotions inside her were so strong that her hands trembled.

"No, you didn't."

"You're the one who never felt good enough. You stupid, macho, jerk. You can't see your own worth, and you put it all on me."

He stood there with her poking at his chest, drenched, with his mouth half open.

Everything she'd gone through in the past months seemed to hit her all at once—her father's death, losing all her belongings, the fear of having to survive on her own after being pampered for so long, Cruz's hostility. She sobbed. "I hate what my father did. I hate that I needed you, but you're right. I did."

His hand rested on her sopping wet back. "Don't do that. Oh man, Gabby, please don't cry."

She couldn't stop. She tried, but she couldn't.

He pulled her against his chest. "Stop." He squeezed her tightly. "I'm glad you needed me. I needed you, too, and I didn't even know it."

She clung to him. They were both soaked, but she didn't care. She needed to be in his arms. He angled his head and kissed her eyes, but she tipped her head back and met his lips, opening herself up to him, holding nothing back.

He ran his fingers into her dripping hair, holding her head securely as he returned her kiss. Without leaving her lips, Cruz lifted her and walked a few steps until her back touched the car. He pinned her, kissed her forcefully, ran his hands across her breasts, ribs, and back. Then clamped his hands onto her hips and stepped back. He breathed as heavily as he had when they'd jogged around the park. He stared at her soaked, plastered clothes.

"Get inside," he said. "I'll look for the keys." He found them quickly and walked around to the driver's side.

Once in the car, he took off his shirt and reached for his bag in the back seat. He pulled out a towel and some clothes. Gabriela took her top off. He glanced at her bra, which was almost see-through and molded to her breasts. He swallowed and handed her a towel and one of his T-shirts.

She took both, put on the dry clothes, and, under the T-shirt, took off her bra.

His pants came off then, and she stared, unashamed, enthralled at the full erection in his wet, royal blue shorts. He placed his thumbs on the waistband and glanced at her. "I'm, ah . . . everything's wet. I gotta take it all off."

Everything? Should she offer to help? She wanted to see him, touch him. She was soaked, too. Maybe they should both take everything off and stay that way. Find something other than clothes to keep each other warm.

He waited.

She turned to the back seat and got her own pair of shorts from her bag as he finished changing. Maneuvering in such a small car took talent. Not looking his way took all her self-control.

He sighed when he was finished dressing and had a pile of wet clothes in a plastic bag he'd taken from his duffle. "Okay, hear me out, Gabriela. I loved your father; you've got to understand. I believed everything he told me about you. I thought he was a great guy." Cruz's voice was quiet and full of pain.

She slipped on her shorts and stared out the window, feeling drained.

"He was the only person I knew who gave money to charities all the time." Cruz continued. "He wrote monthly checks to the American Cancer Society and helped out literacy groups in the Latino communities. Did you know that?"

She did, but she didn't answer or look at Cruz. That didn't make him great in her eyes. Inside, he was a cold, emotionless human being. He'd rejected a young child who'd lost her mother and needed him desperately. He could never see past his own pain to comfort her.

"And he helped me personally. He helped me apply for college and student loans. He paid me more than he should have to drive his car, that's for sure." His voice dropped to almost a whisper. "He even paid for my mother to have an operation once and wouldn't accept repayment."

Cruz stopped talking, and Gabriela turned her head and looked at him, amazed at what she was hearing. Had her father really taken such an interest in Cruz. "Why?"

"He told me I was just like him when he came to this country. He told me that he admired how hard I worked. He . . .."

"What?" Gabriela whispered; tears flowed freely again, and she didn't care if he saw.

"Nothing, he—"

"He told you he wished you were his son rather than—"

"No, he never said that—"

"But he felt it." Gabriela straightened in her seat and wiped her eyes. "I know he did." Maybe he saw himself in Cruz or the son he'd never had. Someone he could care for that didn't look like his dead wife.

Cruz nodded, touched her shoulder. "He was a great man to me. When he talked about how terrible you were, how could I not believe him?"

"I *was* a terrible teenager. I hated him."

"You were crying out for attention."

She sniffed and pulled down the mirror on the sun visor. "I look like shit."

"You look beautiful."

She glanced at him and smiled. "You're a lot nicer than you let on. No wonder Dad loved you."

"He loved you too, Gabriela. He told me so."

She laughed, a weak half-sobbing cackle. "He was probably trying to prove what a wonderful father he was."

Cruz touched her face. "Those were the last words he said to me before he died."

She frowned at him, incredulously. "You were there?"

Cruz nodded.

Gabriela stared at him, then hugged him impulsively, wrapping her arms around his broad torso. She didn't know if she believed Cruz, but she loved him for trying to make her believe that her father cared for her.

Cruz held her patiently and rubbed her back with soothing strokes.

It felt so marvelous to be held, to be so close to this man who both made her blood boil with anger and her flesh blush with desire.

"Cruz, I want to make love to you," she whispered.

He pulled back. "What?"

"I don't mean now. I don't even mean it has to happen. I just want you to know I want you with all my heart. I want to be in your arms and to feel your body loving mine. And it has nothing to do with our business relationship or how needy you think I am."

He kissed her lips. "Ah, Gabriela. You just lowered the green flag, you know?"

"I know. I need to be with you. I've wanted you for so long, Cruz, but I'm terrified. I don't want things to change between us."

He nodded. "I know. This isn't what either of us has wanted."

"No. We want to finish the season and go our separate ways."

"I don't want that, Gabby. Not anymore." He eased her down onto her seat, his lips claiming hers at the same time. He shifted his body and swung his legs over to her side. His full weight held her down, pushing his arousal below her belly. She'd wanted to reach out and touch it through his shorts a few minutes ago; now, she wanted to feel it inside her body. She didn't care about consequences, not about tomorrow or the rest of the season—she just wanted Cruz.

She slipped her fingers through his wet hair, sinking deeper into the sensual kiss. His hands held her shoulders tightly, so she reached for one and guided it to her left breast. His hand covered it, feeling and learning. The warm heaviness of his palm made her nipples painfully harden. He abandoned her breast only momentarily to reach under her top and slip his hand on her skin, taking her nipple between his second and third finger.

She moaned.

He ended the kiss. "No, there won't be any good-byes with us." He worked down her jaw line. "I want you always beside me." Down her neck. "Always."

"Oh, Cruz." Physically, she wanted him, maybe even emotionally, but a strange trepidation made her hands tremble as she held his shoulders. What did he mean by always?

He took her nipple in his mouth as she knew he would. God help her, she wanted him. Was this where it would happen, in her car? How appropriate for the two of them. Was she ready?

He tugged and kissed her nipple until she thought she'd cry out. Then he moved to the other one and repeated the sensual stimulation that had her trembling all over with need.

She felt a jolt run through him just before he lifted his head to look at her. He slid over her, rubbing his lower body provocatively across hers. His lips hovered over hers. "You've changed your mind too, *Querida*? You're ready to give me your heart?"

She stared at him, feeling so confused. She wanted him more than she had ever wanted anything in her life. Except for her independence, she wanted *that* more. She was just starting to find herself in life. For once, she depended on no one. She couldn't let a few moments of ecstasy change the direction of her life. Should she tell him, warn him that sex was all she could offer him right now? He'd once told her that if he slept with her, it would be for real. What did that mean?

Time seemed to stand still as they held each other, and their breaths mingled. Was he waiting for her to say something?

She slid her fingers along the back of his neck. "It's okay, Cruz. Don't stop."

"Of course, I'm going to stop."

She shook her head. "Why?"

He sighed. "Because you're not kidding when you say you're terrified. I see it in your eyes."

But she could do it. She could share physical pleasure with him and not let it affect their future. She wanted to do it.

"And besides, I'm not going to make love to you for the first time in a car, especially when you're feeling so rotten."

She slid one hand down the plane of his face to touch his lips with her fingertips. "Rotten is not how I would describe how I'm feeling right now."

His gaze burned through her, not needing to say anymore. He wanted her to be sure, and she was; she wanted him, but she wasn't sure how much more of her he expected. This was too new; they had to take it slower and make sure they each understood what the other wanted. "You're right," she said. "I need time."

He nodded and pushed off her, replacing the key on the tray between the seats and started the car, and this time, she didn't say a word when he put the car in drive. He drove through the rest of the storm and all the way to Washington without stopping.

She didn't celebrate with him or the team that night after he won the Washington race, nor did she attend many of the practice sessions in the following weeks.

But the distance did nothing to mitigate the burning need she had inside for this man or the knowledge that she was deeply in love with Cruz Ortega, and she was unwilling to pursue that to its eventual end.

CHAPTER FIFTEEN

September

As the checkered flag went down over Cruz's car at the Rocky Mountain Raceways in Salt Lake City, Gabriela jumped into Flip's arms. He twirled her around with the strength of a twenty-year-old. Cruz had just secured his first-place position. Not only was he ahead in points of Brook's car number 45, but now he was two wins ahead. With only two races to go before the end of the season, Cruz was sure to win at least one and stay ahead.

In pit row, the entire team hugged each other, patting backs and kissing Gabriela on her cheek or forehead. Danny even kissed her lips. She was so happy, it didn't matter.

As soon as Cruz came in, he was swarmed by reporters and cameras. Answering her own share of questions, she was kept away from doing the one thing she was dying to do—congratulate Cruz. She searched out his eyes, and he glanced at her over the shoulder of an ESPN reporter and, for the first time in almost a month, allowed their eyes to remain locked for more than a fleeting second. He pointed to the garage, and she nodded.

Flip had opened a few bottles of champagne. She picked one up and headed to the garage to meet with Cruz in private. The others would be there eventually, but at least she'd have a couple of minutes alone with him.

She didn't wait long before she saw him strutting over. His walk was sure and slightly cocky, and that brought a smile to her face. His overly confident attitude sometimes got on her nerves, but today, she didn't mind. What was wrong with a sexy man knowing what he had to offer? She wanted to bind herself to him and share this victory.

"Well, boss, what do you say?" He stopped only inches from her.

She held up the opened champagne bottle. "Congratulations."

He closed his fingers around her hand and brought the bottle to his lips. He took one long swallow. Sweat and dirt covered his face. This would be a turn-off to most women, but he only attracted her more today. He looked like a man who'd worked hard to achieve his goal. Gabriela couldn't be prouder of him.

She walked up against his body, placed her uncaptured hand on his shoulder, and tilted her face. They stared at each other, ignoring all the voices, music, and sounds of motors outside the garage.

"Are you going to take the congratulatory kiss or not?" she asked.

"*Hora mismo.*"

He took the champagne bottle out of her hand and wrapped his arm around her waist. Their lips met, clashed, and Gabriela tasted the iced champagne on his tongue as he plunged it inside her mouth. She tasted strength and victory. She felt power and the kind of spark inside that tempted this man to drive a car with a seven-hundred horsepower engine at almost two hundred miles per hour.

He held her tight as he kissed her lips, bit and tugged at her tongue. Gabriela's whole body awakened, and she felt as if every nerve ending were aroused.

Melting into him, she kissed him back just as passionately, sliding her lips against his. She dug her fingers into his shoulder and pressed her body against his. None of it was enough. Avoiding him, avoiding *this,* had only made her need him more.

"Whooo, hooo," Danny's voice came from the edge of the garage. "Now that's what I call a kiss."

Cruz pulled back and drew a deep, ragged breath. He shifted his gaze to the intruder. "If you say a word to anyone about this, you're fired," he said to Danny.

Danny laughed. "You're not the boss. You can't fire me."

Gabriela took the champagne bottle back from Cruz and took a long drink, needing to cool down. As she drew it away from her mouth, she looked at Danny. "If you say anything to anyone about this, you're fired," she repeated and handed Danny the bottle as she walked out of the garage.

She heard Danny's laughter behind her. She was a crazy woman. What was she doing kissing Cruz that way? If they had been alone, that would have never stopped with a kiss. Never.

Cruz knocked on her hotel door and entered when she opened it. "Everyone's going out tonight. Want to go?"

She returned to folding her clothes into her travel bag. "Not tonight. Thanks anyway."

He closed and locked the door. Gabriela heard the lock but pretended not to notice. She looked up and smiled, not wanting to be alone with him. Was she actually trembling?

"That kiss in the garage—," he began.

"I'm sorry. I was excited about the win. You were incredible. Again."

He stepped up beside her with a sympathetic look. "Uh huh. If you don't want to talk about it—."

"I don't." She loaded her stack of neatly folded clothes into her black nylon bag

He placed a hand on her right shoulder and then his lips on the back of her neck.

She held her breath. "Cruz, don't."

"I can't even stand beside you anymore without hardening instantly. I walk around with a permanent erection."

"Please."

"It's the truth. I look at you, Gabriela, and man, I can't think straight. I can't go on like this."

She grabbed her bag hastily and placed it on the floor beside the bed. She ached to be with him, but . . .. "Go out with the guys, Cruz."

He took her arm. "Did you hear what I said?"

She bit her lower lip and nodded.

"Tell me what you really want. It's time."

She tugged her arm from his grip, then sat on the bed and stared at her trembling knees. "Tonight, we got carried away, that's all."

"That's bull. You can keep trying to fool yourself, but don't try to fool me. What are you afraid of, Gabby? Tell me."

"We've got two more races, then we go our separate ways, remember?" She looked up at him.

He placed his hands in his pockets. She could see the large bulge in his jeans and had to suppress a moan.

"Do we?" he asked. "Go our separate ways, I mean? We don't have to."

"With our success, I can sell this team if you want to keep racing. Or we can close it all down. We'll each have the funds to pursue our real dreams."

His face darkened. "I guess I'd forgotten. We've been doing so well, and I thought. . . ." He stopped talking and looked away, inhaling deeply. "Why do I always feel like I'm lost in a cloud of smoke when I'm with you? Like there's a crash up ahead, and I'm headed straight toward it."

"You're not. We both want the same thing, but—"

"How the hell do you know what I want? Have you asked me?

"We made a deal. You've honored your part. I'm going to honor mine."

"But things have changed!" His eyes narrowed. "How can you talk about going our separate ways?"

"It's going to happen," she whispered.

He cursed. "What happened to you wanting to make love to me? What happened to the connection we made?"

She shook her head, unable to respond.

"Answer me, Gabriela, for the love of God, before I completely lose it!"

She got on her feet and stared at him, wanting to wrap her arms around him and ease this tension.

"You tell me you want me, that it's not just because we were thrown together by fate, that I should have told you how I felt seven years ago, well now you know. I want you in my bed. I want you in my life. How can you tell me we're going to go back to how it was before we started racing together?"

"Because I don't know what to do with that? I've changed my whole life to give us both the freedom to pursue our own goals. And you did, too. And we're this close to getting everything we want." She shot her index finger and thumb under his nose.

He pulled his hands out of his pockets and ran both hands through his hair. His eyes burned into her as if they were surgical lasers. "But I want *you*. We can leave racing behind, but that doesn't mean we leave each other."

"I want to open an art school. I want to travel. I want my life back."

"Wow," he said. "I'm a fucking idiot."

She lowered her gaze, unable to face his accusatory look. Was she incapable of loving? Had she learned from her father after all? No. No, because she did love Cruz, but didn't know what to do about it. "Damn it, Cruz. You're not an idiot. I want you, too. But aside from racing, our lives don't mesh. I can't change my life for you forever. That's not what I want."

He suddenly reached for her arms and pulled her against his hard body. "Woman, you're infuriating. Open your art school. Travel where you want. But come back to me. Is that so hard?"

Was it that easy? It didn't work for Sheena and Griffin. She got tired of waiting for him to follow his dreams. Resented him. Gabriela closed her eyes and dropped her forehead on his shoulder. Cruz caressed her back. He wasn't a man to sit around and wait for any woman.

"You're . . . shaking, Gabriela." He wrapped his arms around her waist and held her. "Ah, *mi vida*, does love really scare you this much?"

She shook her head and eased back, gazing into his dark eyes. "I can't fight this anymore."

"Good."

She wanted him to hold her, to prove nothing outside the two of them mattered, even though she knew better. "Stay here with me tonight. Make love to me until morning."

He tightened his hold on her. "Just until morning?"

"For starters," she said. She wanted and needed him now. And as long as he didn't expect her to be someone she could never be, they'd get along fine. "And I don't want the guys to know."

The muscle on his jaw jumped, and his eyes seemed to cool. "Are we writing a new contract?"

"We still work together, and—."

"No one has to know," he interrupted, annoyance hardening his voice. "Do I get to add my own rules to this contract?"

She closed her eyes. She sounded like such a bitch. But she was just starting to find herself in life. For once, she depended on no one. She loved him, but her independence was still too fragile. "What do you want?"

He walked her backward toward the bed. "I want you, Gabriela. I've always wanted you. I plan to give you multiple orgasms, and I want you to enjoy each one to the fullest."

She drew a shaky breath. "What else?"

"When I'm inside you, I want you to tell me how you want me. Beg me to finish the race."

She chuckled. "It better not be a race. Okay. Easy. Anything else?"

He ran his fingers through her hair. "Yes, stop chasing me away, Gabriela. It breaks my heart."

"Oh Cruz." She sat on the bed and pulled him over her."

He braced his hands on the bed above her shoulders. "I've wanted this since the day we first met."

"Because I was the boss's daughter?" She teased. He was so focused on succeeding, on attaining the American dream, a small part of her wondered if she was no more than a status symbol for him—a trophy of all he'd accomplished. Not consciously, but beneath all that self-assurance.

"No, because you smiled and kissed me when I was nothing but a poor boy begging your dad for a job. You made me feel like I could have the whole world if I wanted it." He nuzzled her ear. "You still make me feel that way, Gabriela. You bring out the best in me."

God, I love you. She pressed against him. "That's such a great answer. Tell me what else I can do for you, Cruz. I'm ready." She whispered.

His hands cupped her bottom. "I wasn't finished. I also wanted you because you're gorgeous and hot and make my blood burn inside." He began kissing her neck.

Her breathing deepened and became heavier. She ran her hands along his back, wanted to tear his shirt right off him. "Tell me more," she insisted.

He pulled back, stared at her, and chuckled. "Because I always wanted to see that look in your eyes when you were beneath me." He unsnapped and unzipped her shorts and slowly slid his fingers inside, touching her through her panties. "I wanted to hear you beg me to come inside you. And you will, *Querida*. I promise you, you will."

CHAPTER SIXTEEN

Gabriela held his face with both her hands, and looked hard at his lips, his eyes, his soul. She knew he cared for her. And she loved him. If, after the season was over, they moved on with their own lives to follow their individual goals and dreams, it was okay. They would always have tonight, and her body would be all his. Methodically, he began to undress her. Her shorts and her top went first. Then he paused and stared at her as she lay in her panties and bra. He looked like a boy who was making love for the first time. She allowed him to take his time. She placed a hand on the side of his face. He met her eyes, and she smiled, a soft, encouraging gift from her to him.

Cruz kissed her hand. His heart pounded so hard he was afraid he'd have a stroke right there on the bed before they even started. All his fantasizing was over. This was real. After all these years, he was really going to make love to Gabriela. How it happened, he wasn't sure, but he was grateful.

He lowered his head and softly kissed her belly, working his way to her breasts. She raised her chest up off the mattress, and he helped unsnap the bra. Her hands pulled his shirt off at the same time. Her arms wrapped around his neck, and her soft breasts pressed against his hard chest. The puckered tips rubbed his own nipples and sent tiny jolts down his body to his groin. He shrugged off his shirt completely and returned to her, held her, stared at her.

He'd never taken so much time with a woman before in his life, but he wanted this to last forever.

She kissed his jaw. He closed his eyes and turned his head to meet her lips. He kissed her, loving her with his lips.

He couldn't delay any longer. He wanted her now. When he pulled away, she gripped his shoulders. "Wait."

"I'm not going far, querida. But I have to take these jeans off." He slid off the bed and quickly kicked off the jeans and briefs.

Cruz stood naked beside the bed, and it took all her restraint to keep from reaching out to him. He moved over her, and Gabriela reached for his bare chest. He had a small tattoo of a cross on his back, below his left shoulder. She pressed her fingertips to it.

"You found where I've been branded."

"Mmm."

"Like it?"

"Seems a shame to do anything to mar this beautiful body, but who could argue with a cross." Especially since his name in Spanish meant just that: cross.

He smiled and bent his head, taking one of her nipples in his mouth. His hot lips and coarse tongue built explosive sensations inside her. With every tug, she felt an overwhelming urge to have him lie across her, their bodies merging as one.

"Oh, Cruz," she moaned. She kissed his shoulders, chest, and nipples until he looked so on edge that she was sure he'd rip her panty off and thrust himself inside her.

But he playfully pulled them off with his teeth, torturing her with his patience.

He leaned over the bed, then reappeared with a small package. He handed it to her. "Put it on me?"

The anticipation of finally touching him made her fingers tremble. She looked at the individually wrapped condom. "Hot fudge?" She laughed. "What's this?"

"Sorry, I picked it up in Vegas."

She eyed him speculatively. "With me in mind?" An unfair question, but she was curious.

"Absolutely. Who else?"

She nodded, thrilled at the knowledge that he'd been thinking of making love to her for so long. She tore open the package. The scent of chocolate filled the room. "Mmm." She gave him a wicked smile. "I'll never be able to eat chocolate again without thinking of you."

He chuckled and placed a hand on her face. "Sorry, it's all they had."

She touched him, stroking his bare, hot flesh first until his legs trembled. "Don't be sorry, *carino*," she said as she kissed him below the navel. By the time she smoothed the condom over him, he was pulsing and thick, and Gabriela wanted him so bad parts of her throbbed as well. "It looks delicious."

"Come here." He reached for her. "I want you so badly."

"I want you too." But they'd both have to wait just a few minutes longer. She had to have a little taste. She drew his hands away and placed her lips on him.

"Ay Dios," he moaned.

Her tongue ran up the length of him, feeling the contours, tasting pure chocolate.

He arched his body, sank his fingers in her hair. She felt powerful, thrilled that she was able to give him so much pleasure. She continued to lick him. "Mmm, I was right. Delicious."

He groaned. "You're driving me crazy."

She laughed. "That's the idea." Then she took him completely in her mouth, using her tongue and lips, to bring him as much pleasure as he could endure. Finally, in an impatient gesture, he pulled her away and laid her on the bed.

Stretched above her, he moved between her thighs. She immediately wrapped her legs around his waist. The head of his penis just touched her own swollen and waiting body.

He kissed her, his tongue sinking and plunging into her mouth, doing everything she wanted him to do with his erection. She finally broke the kiss and arched her body. "Oh Cruz, *carino, que esperas*?"

"I'm waiting for the right time."

"It was twenty minutes ago."

He chuckled. "No." He slowly began to enter. Moving in, then pulling out. "It was years ago." With every pump, he entered a little more, but not nearly enough.

She scratched his back and reached for his buttocks, anything to make him come fully inside her. "Please, Cruz. I need you so badly."

"Do you, *querida*?"

"Yes, oh, please don't keep me waiting anymore."

He stared into her eyes for a fraction of a second, then began moving quicker and quicker, and with four deep thrusts, Gabriela lost all conscious thought. The tremors passing through her body consumed all her energy, and she could no longer think, only feel Cruz deep inside her—thick and hard.

He'd stopped and let her recover, but having him buried within her body, even motionless, extended her pleasure. Tiny aftershocks followed, leaving her clinging to him.

He kissed her when she calmed. "Shall I go on?"

She nodded. "Mmm. Until morning."

He smiled. "Remember. You asked for this. I intend to continue loving you until you can't stand it anymore."

She pulled his head down and took his lips. She wanted him inside her all night.

However, he began a furious kind of lovemaking that made his slow, methodical love play pale. Gabriela cried out her second release, which left her limp and unable to catch her breath. This time, knowing that Cruz was still rock-hard inside her brought a sense of awe and trepidation. This was a man who could go for hours at speeds which would make a normal person lose consciousness. She knew his willpower.

"You okay?" he whispered.

"I'm not sure."

"One more time?"

She felt like she was on a wild, never-ending ride. "Cruz, *Amor mio*, I can't take much more."

He kissed her forehead and pulled out, laying on the bed beside her.

She was immediately shocked. "I didn't mean—"

"It's okay."

"No, I—"

"I'm not through by a long shot." He smiled. "Just giving you time to rest."

He lay on his back and held her, so her head was nestled on his shoulder. She rested an arm across his chest and made small circles with her fingertips.

"Cruz?"

"Hmm?"

She couldn't tell him she loved him, but she needed to say something. She lifted her body on her elbow and rested her chin on his chest. "How do you feel?"

He smiled. "Like I've died and gone to heaven."

"Me too."

He reached over and touched her hair, his fingers gently caressing her scalp. "I don't ever want to stop making love to you, Gabriela."

She slid above him, not wanting to think about what he meant. "Then don't. Let's keep making love."

He placed his hands on her thighs as she slid onto him. "*Ay, Dios*," he hissed.

"Don't hold back anymore, *carino*, let me feel you let go."

He held her tight. "Are you sure?"

She kissed him softly. "I'm sure."

They made love slowly, holding each other with each thrust, kissing passionately until they convulsed together, their souls mating.

As they lay drained beside each other, Gabriela couldn't have stopped the tears if she had tried. Cruz stared but didn't comment. He left the bed and brought her a glass of water. "Here." He sat beside her.

She sipped the water and it felt wonderful on her hoarse throat. Her tears subsided. She'd never been this moved after being with a man. Cruz touched a place in her heart that no one had ever awakened. She didn't know what to say to him.

He kissed her temple. "Everything will work out."

She handed the glass back. "It already has."

"How about some dinner?" he asked.

She gazed up at him through the blurriness of her tears and smiled. He wasn't even commenting on her stupid sentimentality. Things weren't really all that complicated. Who'd of thought Cruz would end up being this loving? "I'm starving."

Arriving at home and saying goodbye was awkward. They didn't have another race scheduled for about six weeks. He would practice, run small local races as training, but she wouldn't attend those.

He sat on her couch. "Good to be home, isn't it?"

She shrugged and stretched after the long car ride. "This isn't much of a home. It's more like a place I'm stuck at when we're in California."

"Must be hard to get used to after living in your father's big palace."

"I hadn't lived with my Dad in a long time. But the house he'd given me was so nice. I had four bedrooms—one that I converted into an art studio—a beautiful yard with fruit trees. A Jacuzzi . . . I miss it."

He stood. "You'll have those things again someday, Gabriela."

"No, I won't. Who are we kidding? Besides, I don't want what I had with my father."

"You'll have whatever you want. You're amazing."

She smiled and took his hand. The urge to walk into his arms was overwhelming, but she resisted. Their one beautiful night was over, and they weren't a couple. "I'll see you in a few weeks, Cruz."

"I could stay tonight—"

"No." She released his hand and began walking toward her front door. "Our agreement was—"

"You couldn't have been serious about that? You want to pretend nothing ever happened? That we didn't have the most pleasurable, fantastic, blissful night of our lives together?"

She wanted him to stop reminding her. She shook her head. "I'll never forget it."

"You're damn right you won't." His brows were drawn together, and his voice was loud. Then he sighed. "Look, Gabriela, querida." He reached for her.

She pulled back, wanting to make this as painless as possible but also be firm. "I might stop and see your practice runs, but I've got a lot to do in the next few weeks before the Bakersfield race. Let's finish out this season as professionals, okay?"

He stared at her like she was a strange bug from outer space. "You're crazy, Gabriela, you know that?"

Oh, she knew that, all right. "We really don't need distractions, Cruz. You have two more races to win. That's what I want from you."

He stepped away from her, the look on his face a mixture of shock, hurt, and anger. "That's what you want from me?" he repeated the words slowly, furiously.

"Yes, I want the sponsors to feel they've gotten their money's worth this season."

He pulled the door open. "You got it, *Querida*. I'll give you *all* your money's worth." He stormed out, justified in his anger.

CHAPTER SEVENTEEN

October

When the knock on the door interrupted her painting, Gabriela didn't know whether to be grateful or irritated. She put her brush down, wiped her hands, and opened her front door. Danny stood on the other side. Gabriela, immediately looked around to see if anyone else was with him. "Is Cruz okay?" She hated that the first thing she thought of was that he might be hurt.

"Yeah, fine. I just wanted to talk to you for a sec."

"Of course. Come in. Can I get you anything? I don't have much food or anything to drink. I can make coffee."

He shook his head. "I just, ah, wanted to ask you about Sheena."

"Have a seat," she said, pointing to her couch, her heart hurting for him.

He dropped down on the couch. "That last race was awesome, wasn't it?"

"Incredible." She sat beside him.

"He's going to win the series. I just know it."

Gabriela crossed her fingers on both hands. "Let's hope so. Listen, Danny, what you saw the other day between Cruz and me—."

"Oh, shit. I don't care. You walked in on me and Sheena in the storage closet." He laughed. "We're even now."

But she didn't want to be even. "I just don't want you to think, you know."

"That you're together?"

"Yeah, because we're not."

Danny raised an eyebrow. "If you say so. He's . . . ah, I think he's in love with you, Gabriela. It's none of my business. I'm just saying."

She didn't want to talk about Cruz or to ask what made him believe Cruz had feelings for her. "What did you want to ask me about, Sheena?"

He fisted his hands together between his legs, looking sheepish. "Yeah, anyway, Sheena hasn't been back to the garage, and well, we've been traveling a lot. I want to talk to her."

"Danny," Gabriela wasn't sure what to say. "Did you call her?"

"She won't take my calls or respond to my texts."

Gazing at his profile, she wanted to caress his face to ease the anxious lines on his forehead. He had endeared himself to everyone on the team. For Gabriela, he was like a little brother she never had. "What does that tell you?"

"That I'm fucked?"

Gabriela laughed. "Well, I wouldn't have put it that way. She's going through a lot. I don't think she knows what she wants."

He reached for Gabriela's hands and squeezed her fingers. "Can you call her for me? Tell her to come over here. I just want to talk to her."

"I'm not getting involved in this."

"I said some really mean things to her. I was pissed, you know. I didn't know she was planning to marry some other guy."

"I'm sorry, Danny. She should have been honest with you. I think you should move on." She pulled her hands out of his. This was beyond uncomfortable.

"Just call her, please?"

"No. And say what? That you're sitting here, in my house, foolishly waiting for her?"

"Yeah, that will work."

She shook her head and stood. "Danny, I love you. Take it from me, Sheena is not for you."

"You don't know that. Call her. That's all I ask. Please."

"Oh my God." She reached for her purse and pulled out her cell phone. "I can't believe I'm doing this." She planned to spend the day painting, not being a mediator for her best friend and her team's mechanic. She dialed Sheena, who picked up on the second ring.

"Hey, you're back?" She asked.

"Sheena, Danny is in my living room forcing me to call you because you won't return his calls. Come and get him out of my house."

"Is he stupid? It's over."

Gazing at his expectant face, she said, "Apparently not."

"I can't deal with him."

"I warned you this would happen, and you didn't listen to me. Now you have a problem. Get over here."

She sighed. "Okay, fine. I'll be there in an hour."

Gabriela disconnected the call. "She's coming over."

"Yes!" Danny jumped off the couch and smiled like they'd just won another race. "Thank you, Gabriela. You're so awesome. I knew she'd listen to you. Everyone listens to you."

Sure, they do. She reached across and hugged him. "She's going to hurt you. I wish you wouldn't pursue this."

Shaking his head, he dropped a kiss on Gabriela's cheek. "I have to. She's so much fun to be with. She's gorgeous and cool and funny. And she's so talented. She writes these amazing lyrics. I've never met anyone like her. And we get along all the time; we never fight, well, until I found out about her lame boyfriend. But she doesn't love him."

"I know."

"Then she shouldn't be with him."

Well, she wasn't anymore, but Gabriela would let them talk about that. "I'm going to go work on my painting like I was before you barged in here. You can watch TV. The remote's on the table."

Strolling to the other side of the living room where she'd set up a little corner with her art supplies, he looked at the painting. "That's really good. What is it?"

Gabriela laughed. "A thunderstorm."

"With two people embracing?"

"Yeah."

"Wow, kind of dark and disturbing, but evocative."

Gabriela eyed him and lifted an eyebrow. "Nice critique."

He shrugged, then walked away and started rummaging through her kitchen cabinets. Having found some crackers, probably stale, he sat on her couch with his feet on the coffee table to wait for the woman who was not the love of his life.

Sheena arrived almost two hours later, walking in like a tornado unleashing its wrath on Danny. How dare he? Was he that much of a loser? Wasn't he smart enough to realize when he'd been dumped? What they had together was nothing? If he ever tried to contact her again, she was going to file harassment charges.

Gabriela listened in shock and was about to stand up to tell her to stop humiliating him and leave when she stopped on her own.

Danny smiled. "I've missed you so much."

"You're pathetic," Sheena said.

He placed the glass of water on the coffee table and stood. With a big grin, he reached out a hand. "I'm awesome, and you know it. You can't marry some dude who never makes you laugh and is too stupid to realize that you need passion and excitement in your life."

She ignored his hand, but her shoulders lowered. "I'm not going to marry Griffin."

Danny lowered his hand, but his grin widened. "Good girl. I knew you'd come to your senses."

"Shut up. You have no idea what you're talking about. My entire life, as I planned it, has been upended."

"You are so fricken hot." He took a step closer, looking at her adoringly. "And you're going to have a fantastic life. You're talented, and smart, and really hot." He grinned again.

Sheen sighed and glanced at Gabriela as if to say: What do I say to this guy? "Danny, what do you want? Why are you here?"

"I want us to keep hanging out."

"I can't keep hanging out with you. I need to move on with my life."

"Come on. I want to take you motor crossing and to camp out at the river. Oh, and you're going to love Comicon. Remember you said you'd go with me. We can dress up like dragons."

Sheena laughed. "I don't do those things, you fool."

He grabbed the waistband of her jeans and pulled her toward him roughly. "That's why you're so miserable. Kiss me."

And she did. Gabriela couldn't believe it. But she smiled. Who could resist Danny? He was so cute. "Hey, break it up. You're still in my house."

Danny pulled away from the woman whose heart he seemed to have melted. "Sorry, boss. But thank you." He rushed over to her and hugged her, too."

Sheena gazed at her. "What am I going to do with him?"

Gabriela shrugged. "Hang out?"

Laughing, Sheena nodded. "We'll talk later. Right now, I'm going to this kid's house to get reacquainted."

"Alright!" Danny said. "We're out of here."

And they left. Maybe Danny was perfect for her after all. He was so not serious, and in her own way, Sheena was just as pleasure-seeking and aimless. Danny was a hard worker, but not so focused on, well anything, which meant he wasn't likely to neglect Sheena.

Gabriela's heart played a happy beat, and she turned her attention back to her painting. It really was dark, but maybe not so evocative. She stood and drove to the beach, needing a long walk and some fresh air to think about her own mess of a love life. She had a love life now, right? The truth was, she wasn't sure about anything.

Cruz tried not to be openly hostile to Gabriela when she showed up at their local track. He could see in her eyes that she didn't want to be there, but she was being supportive.

She looked incredibly hot in her jeans. All he could think of was how she'd felt in his arms, wrapped around his body, sleeping beside him. He wanted her there again, and it hurt that she was brushing him off. What the hell was she afraid of?

He smiled and sat beside her on the bench in the garage. "You look great."

She smiled back. "Thank you. I've gotten lots of rest, and I needed it. I went for a walk on the beach. I almost called you to come join me."

"I wish you had." He touched her knee. "I've missed you."

"Cruz, I didn't mean to anger you when we returned—."

"Forget it."

"I really want to continue being friends."

He shook his head. She knew better than that. "Sometimes in life, we do things that are irreversible." He got to his feet.

"Cruz, I'm still your boss."

He laughed. "And my lover."

She looked uneasy. "I worked so hard to earn your respect, then blew it all for one night of sex."

Now, he was getting angry. She wanted to pretend that it had been nothing but sex between them? The hell with her. "Naw, querida, my respect for you has only increased. Anyone who can do an all-night marathon with me in bed . . . is impressive. You deserve an award."

She winced. His vulgarity had produced the effect he wanted, but he immediately regretted saying it. Their night together might have been just sex to her, but to him, it had been a magical, sublime experience.

She stood, and he grabbed her wrist. "If you don't want me to reduce it to something cheap, then don't you do it, Gabriela."

She blinked, meeting eyes, and nodded. Then she held a hand to the side of his face, touching him so softly, he thought he'd actually melt. How did she have such a powerful effect on him?

"Fair enough." Her eyes actually started to mist. "But let me go. Don't push for more.

Why did intimacy with him make her cry? A desperate fear that she was slipping away made him soften his tone. "Gabby, you don't always have to be so strong, you know. My arms are ready to hold you any time you want to walk into them."

Her bottom lip trembled. Tears were on the brink of falling. "I want to walk into them so badly, Cruz. I want to wrap myself inside you and stay there, safe and protected. That's why I can't do it. I won't become a weak, needy woman."

He shook his head, unable to comprehend what she was talking about. Did she think letting someone love her made her weak? "You're not making any sense."

"I have to be my own woman. This is the first time in twenty-four years that I haven't had to depend on anyone. When Dad died, I didn't know what to do, how to take care of myself. I never want to feel that helpless again."

His grip softened, his thumb brushing against the soft skin of her inner wrist, attempting to show her the tenderness he felt for her. "But why do you think being with me will make you helpless?"

"Because you're you."

"What the fuck does that mean?"

"You want a woman who stays home and takes care of you and your kids. Didn't you tell me that? You demand that everyone do what you say. Look, Cruz, some women may want to be completely taken care of by their men, but I'll never be that woman."

"What was the other night all about, then?"

"You know what it was about?"

"If you say sex, I swear, I'll walk out of here, and you'll never see me again."

She raised an eyebrow as if challenging him to say it wasn't about sex. They'd been hot for each other for months. But damn it, he didn't want to lose her. "We have two races left. Do you intend to walk away from me when it's all over?"

"I've always intended to sell the team—"

"I'm not asking about the damn team; I'm asking about me!"

"You are the team, I—." She broke off suddenly. "I mean, you're part of the team, and—."

"I've heard enough." He stepped away from her. "Fuck you, Gabriela, and this team. I'm done."

As he headed for his car, he heard her calling him, but refused to turn back around.

"What does that mean?"

He ignored her and kept walking.

"Cruz!

Damn her. His heart ached.

"You can't be *done*. You're under contract."

He paused; his hands closed into fists. Then he kept going. He jumped into his car, gunned the engine of the cheap four-cylinder car, and peeled out of the track parking lot.

What did she expect him to do? Stuff his feelings for her away and pretend they didn't exist? What he wanted was to make love to her day and night. Get a little place together. Spend hours sitting beside her on their patio, watching their kids play on the grass. Yes, it was her face he saw in his dream home. But deep down, she was right; he would want her to be home with those kids, not working, not having a life that didn't include him. He realized how selfish that was, but that's what he wanted.

If Gabriela wasn't the woman for him, then why did it hurt so much to consider life without her?

After his qualifying run in Bakersfield, he sat alone for hours watching everyone except Gabriela leave. She'd walked into the hauling trailer and never came out. He climbed into the trailer. Gabriela was sorting tools, putting them in their proper place, and leaving the mechanic's workbench spotless. She'd gotten into the habit of picking up after the guys. They were probably the tidiest team in the Western series.

She had her back to him. With measured steps, he approached her, then encircled her body with his arms and produced a chocolate bar.

Seemingly startled, she turned her head. "Cruz. You scared me." Then she looked at his offering. She frowned, a smile slowly creeping onto her lips. "What's this?"

"You said you wouldn't ever eat chocolate again without thinking of me." He hoped the images going through her head were as erotic as his.

She turned in the circle of his arms. "Is this what you were thinking about in that car today? Your qualifying run wasn't what it usually is."

He shrugged. "You're all I think about, Gabriela." He stepped closer and braced both his arms on the workbench.

"You're backing me up against something again."

He nodded. "Your only option is to hop up on this bench, wrap your arms and legs around me, and enjoy it."

The defiance on her face grew, making her look strong and sexy. He heard all her protests before she voiced them: not in a trailer, someone could come in, I'm too damn proper to do something like this. But he knew how to quiet every one of her objections. He pressed his hips against hers and angled his face, bringing his lips almost against hers, but he didn't want to kiss her just yet.

She stood motionless. He'd caught her by surprise, and he loved the look on her face right now, tempted, yet cautious. Her eyes shifted over his shoulder to the door.

"Everyone's gone," he said.

She looked at him again. "I'm not about to—."

"Yes, you are."

"Have you gone crazy?"

He grinned and shifted his hips, still the only part of his body touching hers. She placed her hands on his shoulders. *Yes, triumph was moments away.*

"I'm going crazy working with you, beside you, and not touching you. Why did you do this to me, Gabriela? Why did you let me make love to you if this was the way it was going to be between us?"

Her face crumbled. All defiance was gone. "I'm sorry."

"Don't be sorry, damn it, just stop giving me the cold shoulder. I can see in your eyes you want me as bad as I want you." He wrapped his arms around her and lowered his head onto her shoulder.

He planned on seducing her, but all he was doing was clinging to her like a little boy, praying she would hold him and want him as much as he wanted her. Some macho, super stud, he thought in disgust. He was past pretending. He was scared to death she would send him away.

But her arms began to slide down his shoulders, to his back. "You're making me feel guilty," she whispered.

He lifted his head and stared into her eyes. "You should. If I shut you out after that night together, how would you have felt?"

She was silent for a few moments; then, she searched his face. "Used."

He shrugged and couldn't suppress a smile. "Well, I was thinking more along the lines of devastated."

She angled her head and kissed him. The kiss started out sweet, but before long, it became so hot, so wild, they tore away from each other to catch their breath. She pushed him back and pulled open her shirt. "This isn't my style," she said, exposing her lacy, black bra.

"Not mine either." But he'd take her anywhere, anytime.

He unzipped his race suit while she watched. Released his throbbing erection and quickly covered himself with a condom, no chocolate scent this time. Then he gazed at her.

Her eyes were dark, her lashes half-lowered over them. "To hell with style," she said. "Come here."

Cruz reached for her jeans, unsnapped them, and slowly lowered them over her hips and lower still until she stepped out of them. He lifted her. She wrapped her legs around him, as she settled onto his hot penis. Placing her against the wall of the trailer, he plunged into her repeatedly, needing to ease some of the tension inside him. She held onto his shoulders as she kissed the side of his neck, releasing heavy, gasping breaths.

Cruz slowed his rhythm. "Oh, Gabby, I need you so much." She tossed her head back, and he kissed her neck. "So much," he repeated.

She let out a plaintive cry and clutched harder at his shoulders. "Cruz, Cruz. . . ." She repeated his name again and again, and it filled him with pride and excitement to hear her speak his name with such passion as she trembled in his arms, her body milking his penis with each contraction.

She lunged forward, her forehead touching his. "I needed this, too. I thought you were going to leave and not come back. I didn't sleep all night. Worrying."

He kissed her temple. "I'm never leaving you."

She found his lips somehow and lavished a passionate, erotic kiss. He met her tongue as she opened her mouth wider, then caught it between his teeth momentarily. She moaned, and slowly he released her tongue and stroked it with his lips instead.

She shuddered and clutched him to her breasts. Cruz drove into her, faster and harder and came in an explosive, violent rush that left him weak. He held her tight so he wouldn't drop her, but he had to let her slip down.

"You okay?" He asked, slightly lightheaded.

"Yeah." She shifted out of his grasp, already dressing.

He closed his eyes. Maybe this hadn't been the best place to make love to her, but he had to possess her again, touch her, make her realize he was the only man for her. He pulled his clothes back on and went to her. Running his finger along her jawbone, he searched her eyes.

"I can't give you what you had with your father, Gabby, but I can make you happy."

She tried to turn her face, but he held her chin in place.

"I can't make *you* happy, don't you see?" she said and pushed him back.

"Why don't you let me decide that?" he said to her back. She stood at the workbench, reaching for tools again, just as she had been when he walked in—as if he hadn't even touched her.

She slammed down a wrench and faced him. "Everything you thought about me at the start of the season was true. I only care about myself. I want the most money for the least amount of work, and what I miss most about my father is his money."

She looked like a frightened little girl. "Come on, Gabby." She'd spent months showing him how wrong he'd been about her, so why was she saying this now?

"It's true. I was spoiled and pampered and—."

"And not loved."

Tears sprung to her eyes. She attempted to walk past him, but he grabbed her arm.

"Let me go," she cried.

"That's why you cried in my arms when we made love. Because it's the first time you felt someone truly love you. And I do, Gabriela. I am deeply in love with you."

If her wide eyes and shocked expression were anything to go by, he'd guess his declaration of love was as unexpected to her as it was to him.

"You can have your own career; you can have kids or not; you can spend every penny we make; you can do anything you like, Gabby, as long as it's with me." He took a deep breath and pulled her closer.

She clung to him without speaking.

"But you have to make up your mind now, Gabby. I won't be a puppy dog following behind you, waiting for a few scraps. Take all of me, one hundred percent. Or none of me."

Tears flowed down her face, but she had an incredulous look in her eyes. "You're not a guy to follow a woman around. You'll get tired of me."

"You can't get tired of your wife."

"Are you asking me to *marry* you?" She said it as if it were a bad word.

"Yeah, I guess I am. As soon as you're ready."

She shook her head. "I'll never be ready. I—."

The door to the trailer flew open. “Cruz,” Felipe called breathlessly. “Call from Mexico, Amigo. Your mother’s in the hospital.”

Cruz shot out the door and ran to the main office. *God no, not his mother again.*

When Gabriela reached the office, Cruz’s shoulders were hunched, and his head rested low on his forearms. He still held the receiver in his right hand. She wondered if he was crying and didn’t know what to do. Slowly, she walked up behind him and placed a hand on his shoulder. “Cruz?”

His back straightened, and he hung up the phone. “She had a massive stroke. Probably won’t make it. My dad tried to reach me on my cell, but I was—my phone is turned off.”

A lump made swallowing impossible. She settled for a deep breath. “I’ll make plane reservations for you to go to her.”

He nodded absently.

The sound of Flip clearing his throat came from the door. “Hate to say this, but what about tomorrow’s race?”

“We’ll pull out,” Gabriela said.

Cruz stood abruptly. “No. I’ll race, then fly home.” He gave Gabriela a cold, sharp look. “I want to make sure you have enough money to sell the team at the end of the season. Then we can each go on with our own lives, just like we agreed.”

CHAPTER EIGHTEEN

Gabriela could barely function on race day. She'd slept miserably; her eyes burned from lack of rest and crying. Too much happened too fast. Wild sex with Cruz, his marriage proposal, his mother's stroke. She wanted to talk to him but knew it wouldn't be anytime soon.

As she watched him suit up and the guys prepare the car, she tried to get herself into the spirit of the day. The next to the last race. Cruz could end up winning the ARCA-Menards series. But she wasn't excited. She didn't want to be here at the Bakersfield track, where they'd started this journey together.

But they were, and Cruz seemed determined to race today.

Cruz tried to keep his vision from blurring as the opening ceremonies began. He didn't sleep last night. The hours he hadn't spent on the phone with his father, he'd spent thinking of Gabriela. To be turned down flat when you told a woman you loved her and wanted to marry her, was enough to deflate any man's ego. But the pain was twice as sharp for him because he'd never thought he was in her league in the first place.

The national anthem was sung, the teams introduced, and now it was time to get in the car. He wanted to get this race over with. His father needed him, and Cruz had to hold his mother's small, wrinkled hand in his once more.

Flip patted his shoulder. "You okay, boy?"

Cruz nodded.

As they followed the pace car out, he forced himself to think of nothing but the race. He wove back and forth, heating his tires for more traction. As they came out of corner two, Cruz punched and poked at the accelerator, making the car lurch forward in spurts. Everything worked perfectly.

When the pace car veered off, Cruz punched the accelerator and began the battle for fifth place. Before completing two laps, the caution flag fell.

"Shit," Cruz shouted. He didn't need delays, damn it.

"Take it easy," Flip said through the headset.

As soon as the green flag allowed them to restart, Cruz charged ahead, taking the fourth spot.

He kept up consistent speed for the next twenty laps or so; then, another caution flag dropped just as he'd moved around car 27 and took the third spot. But the time was perfect.

"I'm coming in. The left front tire's going down."

The pit crew went to work changing four tires with an air pressure adjustment, and then Cruz restarted in third position. He quickly came up to the bumper of car 99. "I've got 'im," Cruz said.

"That's fine, but don't overdrive," Flip warned.

He followed him for three laps, and then car 99 hit oil, sending him on a wild ride.

"Stay out of his way," Flip shouted.

"I can get around him."

"No. Don't try it."

"I'm going for it."

"Damn it, Cruz."

Cruz charged forward, passing car 99 and taking the second position.

"You stubborn son of a bitch," Flip muttered.

Cruz ignored him and stepped on the accelerator. He wanted this race to be over. Visions of his mother kept interrupting his driving. Memories of being a young boy in Mexico, of depending on her for nourishment, for nursing his scrapes and bruises, for mending his broken heart. Of course, even his mother couldn't mend his heart this time. Gabriela had taken it and ripped it to shreds.

Halfway through the race, Cruz was tired, emotionally a wreck, and he had to force himself to concentrate.

"You just got bumped," Flip said through his headphones.

"Tell me about it. He nudged my bumper, trying to pass me."

"Keep at it. You got 'im."

Cruz was at top speeds, his right foot trembled, and his leg threatened to cramp from the pressure. He placed his left foot over on top of his right to keep it from involuntarily lifting off the accelerator.

"Damn, he scraped my side," Cruz called.

"Careful, you got the curve coming."

Cruz could feel car 99 inching up his right side. He didn't want to lose his number two spot. He turned to the right, cutting his opponent off, but began to lose control. The air was lifting his front end. Damn, he saw the curve coming too fast. Turned quickly left. More lift. He punched the gas pedal, but nothing seemed to help.

He heard Flip in his ear, speaking rapidly, but couldn't comprehend the words. He was knocked into the front stretch wall and flopped on his side. All he could do now was hold on. He was T-boned and sent spinning. Then, everything went black.

Gabriela hugged her arms together, tighter and tighter as the doctor spoke to her and Flip. Cruz had been lucky. He suffered a broken shoulder blade and a bruised sternum. He'd be okay. Gabriela exhaled—a gush of air, leaving her limp with relief. When the rescue crew reached the crushed car lying on its roof with two wheels still spinning, and she hadn't seen any movement inside, she'd nearly died. She wanted to climb over the pit crew wall and run out there. The guys held her in place, and Flip actually led her to the back, off the track.

"Calm down," he'd said. "Cameras will be on you; they can't see you fall apart."

"I don't care," she'd cried.

"He'll be okay," Flip promised.

Now it seemed Flip was right. "Can I see him?" She asked the doctor.

"Only for a few minutes."

Tears returned when she saw Cruz looking so fragile. She walked to the side of his bed and touched his forearm gently.

He opened his eyes and took her hand. "Gabby, I need to get home, my mom—," he winced and shifted in bed. The pain was probably unbearable.

Gabriela squeezed his fingers. "You'll be out of here soon."

He nodded. "I don't want her to die without me. I need to see her one more time."

Those damn tears. She wiped them away. "Probably a day or two, and then you can go."

"It might be too late by then."

She shook her head to give him hope, but inside, she feared the same. As a child, she'd watched her mother wither away and never knew which would be the last day she'd see her alive. No one should have to suffer that kind of torture.

"Sorry I ruined the car." His voice was deep and raspy.

She frowned and sniffled. "Forget the car, forget racing. It's over. You'll never have to get in a race car again. I promise."

He closed his eyes. "I lost control, I . . . ." His words faded.

"I'll leave you to rest now."

She started to pull her hand free, but he gripped her fingers. "Gabby," he whispered and opened his eyes just a slit.

"I'm here."

"Go to Mexico for me. Tell my mom I love her."

She felt as if a blast of icy wind had hit her. "Cruz, you—"

"Please, go." He closed his eyes again. "Tell her I'm on my way. To wait.

Gabriela stood as she was, frozen, staring at him. How could she go to Mexico? She didn't even know where his family lived? They didn't know her? Cruz was delirious. She kissed his forehead and slipped out of the room.

In the lobby, she pulled out the airplane ticket which left for Mexico in the morning. She did know where they lived, at least the address, she'd made the reservations, but . . . to go to Mexico and meet Cruz's family at such a grievous time. . . .

She glanced over her shoulder at the closed door. God, she had almost lost him today. Watching the car spin out of control, all those cars slamming into his, the wall of smoke . . . her stomach heaved. What a helpless feeling to watch as someone you love is being taken away in an ambulance.

She placed the plane tickets back in her purse and drew a deep, steadying breath. She loved Cruz; there was no denying it.

If he wanted her to go to Mexico for him, she'd go. And as soon as she got the chance, she'd tell him how much she truly loved him.

Gabriela called and spoke to one of Cruz's cousins to tell him she was on her way, and he arranged for a car to meet her at the airport. They drove about four hours to a small village, which still had many dirt roads. She wasn't able to communicate with her driver, so she admired the scenery of the Mexican countryside. Mexico City was like any city: large and congested. But as they made their way into the suburbs and then the villages, a whole new world emerged.

On the front porch of Cruz's home, a group of family members waited for her arrival. Men and women alike greeted her with a kiss on the cheek.

She recognized Cruz's father immediately, an older, slightly beaten version of Cruz himself.

"I'm so sorry for your suffering," she said, knowing what having a wife and son in the hospital must be doing to him.

Beto Ortega embraced her. "Thank you for coming. My Cruz is going to be okay?"

Gabriela nodded. "He needs to spend a couple more days in the hospital healing, but he'll be fine."

The older man nodded. "Come inside. The women have prepared food for you."

And indeed they had. They prepared enough food to feed twenty people for a whole week. Huge pots of beans and rice covered the stove, and along the horseshoe counter top were dishes of casseroles, guacamole, and salsas. The kitchen looked like a delicious buffet.

"*Tome un poco de Caldo de Res,*" a young woman said.

Even with Gabriela's weak Spanish, she understood she was being offered beef soup.

"*No, gracias,*" Gabriela said, knowing she wouldn't be able to stomach food, even home-cooked, heavenly food like theirs, until she rested. "Later, maybe."

Gabriela settled her suitcase in a small room. A twin bed, a small desk, and a dresser were crammed inside. This was Cruz's childhood room. She smiled, thinking of Cruz as a boy.

She sat on the bed to gather her thoughts for a few minutes. "Oh, Cruz, I hope you make it in time." She knew how important it was for him to see his mother alive one more time. She thought of her own mother and how she missed her. Poor Cruz. Losing your mother was always painful, no matter the child's age. She wept for Cruz and, strangely enough, for herself as well. How she wished, still, that she'd had the opportunity to grow up with two loving parents.

As she wiped her eyes, Gabriela did something she hadn't done since her own mother was sick and on her deathbed. She dropped to her knees and prayed everything would turn out all right.

Cruz's first stop when he entered his hometown was the hospital. When he walked into her hospital room and saw her looking so small on the bed, he felt as if he'd hit a wall in his race car—scared, angry, a crazy feeling of desperation. He inhaled sharply, finding it difficult to breathe.

The nurses told him before he entered that his mother probably would not recover from the stroke. Still, he'd hoped they were wrong. But they weren't. Deep down in his gut, he knew she would be gone soon, and he wanted to shout at the top of his lungs for God to wait. Not yet. She was too young, not even sixty yet. How unfair. Cruz wasn't even married yet. She hadn't held her first grandchild.

He sat beside her hospital bed, kissed her wrinkled arm, and pressed his forehead to her hip.

He cried silently.

She'd lived a full life, took care of the family, his friends, strangers, animals. She'd rise early every morning to prepare breakfast for him and his father and stayed up late every night to make sure the house was spotless. How he'd missed being cared for. He should have been here taking care of her at the end.

He lifted his face and wiped his tears. "I'm sorry, Mamá," he whispered. He kissed her hand and stared at her face. She looked peaceful, as if she were only sleeping rather than in a coma. He remembered when her hair was a deep black, not a mixture of black and gray. Was it only twenty years ago when she worried about a few wrinkles on her face? He reached across and ran his fingertips over a face now carrying all the wrinkles of a long, hard life. She was still beautiful. Always had been.

Worn out, he leaned back in his chair and continued to hold her hand. He'd forgotten to take his painkillers, and his shoulder ached. They wanted him to stay in the hospital one more day, but he refused. "I crashed, big time," he said to his mother. "I'm okay, but the car is nothing but junk metal now." Why was he telling her about that? He hadn't come all this way to talk about race cars.

He sighed and focused on their hands. "I was worried about you and upset about Gabriela. I didn't get enough rest, and well . . . I blew it." He lifted his gaze, looking at his angelic mother. He could picture her shaking her head and murmuring sounds of disapproval.

"Remember, I told you about Gabriela? You suggested I tell her I loved her. I did, but it didn't do any good. She's, ah . . . ." He paused and smiled at his mother's motionless face. "She's scared, Mamá. I guess being stuck with me the rest of her life is a scary thought."

He turned slightly and leaned close to his mother's face. No longer interested in talking about his life. "How am I going to live without you?" He closed his eyes and shook his head, tears spilling again. "Who will I talk to? I'll be lost without you." When he lifted his head and looked at her again, he was staring straight into her open, milk chocolate-brown eyes.

Cruz didn't move a muscle. He looked into her eyes, wondering if she was actually conscious. He wanted to speak but was unable. Instead, their eyes remained locked together, and they spoke without words. All the love, all the tenderness he'd ever received from her, was there again as if he were being bathed in peace and love. He continued to look into her eyes for endless minutes, communicating in a way that seemed almost mystical. He knew how she felt, knew everything she'd say to him if she could. Some things were unexplainable.

"I love you," he whispered finally.

She closed her eyes, and he closed his.

CHAPTER NINETEEN

"*Mi'jo, mi'jo,*" his father's voice kept calling him, but he didn't want to respond. "Cruz, wake up."

Cruz opened his eyes, startled. Where the hell was he? His eyes focused on his mother. He reached for her hand and found it cold, and withdrew it violently. He turned his head and saw his father and Gabriela standing beside him.

Cruz straightened in his chair. Pain shot through his shoulder to his neck, then his head. "Ah, damn."

Gabriela took his hand. "Let me help you."

He looked at her, so grateful she was here. He loved this woman. He wanted her forever. Maybe he didn't deserve her, but he would convince her to love him back. He'd wait until she was ready. Patience, that's what his mother always told him. He wrapped his unbruised arm around her waist and let her help him stand. "Thanks."

"When did you get here?" Gabriela asked.

The clock on the nightstand indicated only two hours had passed since Cruz had arrived at his mother's bedside. "Not too long ago." He released Gabriela and turned to his father.

Beto touched Cruz's face and brushed permanent grease-stained fingers into his hair. "The hospital called me an hour ago. The nurse came in and found . . . she didn't want to wake you, but . . . your mother's gone, you know."

Cruz looked at his mother. He didn't know, but he nodded. Maybe he did know. "She opened her eyes as I talked to her." His voice choked, and he looked at his father, who was remarkably calm. "She knew I was here."

Beto smiled. "She waited for you, *Hijo*." With hunched shoulders and slow steps, Beto sat beside her bed.

"I know," Cruz whispered to himself and bent over the bed to kiss his mother's cheek. *"Adios, Mamá.* Rest in heaven now."

He backed away and reached again for the other woman he loved in this room. "Come on," Cruz said to Gabriela, and they both walked out of the room, leaving Beto to say goodbye in private.

Cruz pulled Gabriela into an embrace as soon as they were out the door. He needed her. Her arms wrapped around him and held him close. Being in her arms felt so right. "Thanks for coming," he said.

"You don't have to thank me."

He let her go and stepped away, drawing a deep breath. "She died in front of me, Gabby. Just like your dad." He pinched the bridge of his nose and shut his eyes tight. No more damn tears. "I'm going to pay the hospital bills and make some, ah, arrangements."

"Bills are paid, Cruz."

He halted and frowned. "They are?"

She nodded.

"Don't tell me my dad—"

"I took care of everything. I didn't want you to have to worry."

"You?" The unexpected kindness of her gesture caught him completely by surprise.

"Your family was sitting around the living room trying to pool their money together, talking about what they would sell, all the while your father sat alone in his chair, his hands glued to his forehead. It was heart-breaking." She blinked watery eyes. "So, I told them you asked me to cover it."

Thoughts of Carlos Alende paying for his mother's bypass came to mind. Then Flip's comment about her being so much like her father. Perhaps she was. "Good thinking. Thank you. I'll write you a check when we get home."

She shook her head. "It's a gift. I don't want you to pay me back."

He rolled his neck to ease the tension. His shoulder ached, feeling almost numb now. He gazed at Gabriela. How had he been lucky enough to cross paths with a creature so lovely and so tenderhearted? He was positive the Alendes, both father and daughter, were his personal angels. He touched her arm. "Gabriela, you don't have any money to—."

"I had enough. Can we drop it, please?"

He frowned again. He wouldn't let her pay his bills, but he nodded. "Yes. Let's leave now, okay?"

The next couple of days were spent on funeral and burial arrangements. They were some of Cruz's darkest days. His only bright spot stood beside him the entire time—Gabriela. They didn't talk about personal matters. His marriage proposal went unmentioned. The time and place weren't right. Yet each time she touched him, held his hand, brought him a drink or food, he thought of that day. He'd pushed her, hadn't asked her properly.

But he would. The next time, when he asked her to be his wife, he'd give her reasons to say yes.

After the burial service, family members congregated at his father's house. Beto sat alone in the courtyard he and Cruz had built together out of stones and rocks. The fountain they'd bought their mother one Christmas stood beautifully in the middle. The sun overhead reflected brightly off the cascading water.

Cruz sat beside his father on the bench. "I can move back home."

Beto looked momentarily startled, then gripped Cruz's knee. *"Hola, Hijo."*

"We can work together like we used to."

Beto laughed. "I thought you were a man now."

"I am, Papi, but—"

"Men must build their own lives."

Cruz swallowed through the tightness in his throat. He nodded. "I don't want you to be alone." The words came out like a choked whisper.

"I'm never alone." Beto patted his knee and then withdrew his hand. "So, tell me about this beautiful woman you sent us."

Cruz stared at the cracks on the old rocks by his feet. "Didn't *Mamá* tell you?"

He nodded. "Do you want to marry her?"

"*Si*, so badly I ache inside."

"How about those race cars?"

The quick change in subject when he'd just revealed how much he wanted a woman confused him. He looked at his father, searched his face for understanding, but found none. "I, I like those too, but I'm going to begin my career as an accountant soon."

Beto stared intently at him, the wrinkles on his brown weathered face made him look more severe than he was. "Why?"

"What do you mean, 'why?' It's a good career, what I've been studying to become for years." His father used to be so perceptive; why was he so obtuse today?

"Do what makes you happy, *Hijo*."

Cruz swallowed and nodded. "Having a clean, respectable job will make me happy."

"The only response that came from here," Beto tapped him at the center of Cruz's chest, "was the answer about the girl. Not the cars, not the accounting career."

Cruz took his father's hand. He should have known. The old man was taking him apart piece by piece, like he did the engines of cars, until he found the problem. He was right, of course. He had no passion for accounting, and the passion he'd developed for racing came from Gabriela. She was what he loved and wanted most in the world. "Some things aren't so easy to get."

"Of course not. You think it was easy to convince your mother to marry me?" He snorted. "Never worked harder at something in my life."

Cruz was surprised. His mother had been so devoted to Beto. How amazing to think there had been a time when she didn't love him. He smiled. "That Ortega charm got her, huh?"

Beto shook his head, a soft smile on his lips. "Women aren't impressed by charm for long. You know how to capture her heart, *Hijo*. You don't need advice from an old man like me." He squeezed Cruz's hand and released it, then patted the back of his head like he used to when Cruz was a kid.

Cruz laughed.

"You make me proud. And maybe give me some grandkids. Your mother made me promise to ask you to give us grandkids."

Cruz rolled his eyes. Gabriela didn't want kids. She'd made that clear. But she was only twenty-four. "We'll see."

From the corner of his eye, he saw a movement at the door. He turned and saw Gabriela standing on the back porch. He stood. "Hey."

"Sorry, I didn't know you two were out here."

"Come on out."

Beto stood as well. "Yes, please. I need to go inside and let people console me." He walked slowly away and kissed Gabriela when he reached her. "You see, kids. When you love someone as long as I have, something like death can never separate you. But . . . ." He shrugged. "It helps them to fuss over me a while." He continued to the house.

Cruz held out a hand. Gabriela walked to him almost shyly.

"I called Flip last night and told him to buy a new car," he said.

She paused, withdrawing the hand she was about to clasp to his. "What?"

"We need a car for the last race."

She shook her head. "No more races."

"One more."

"Why?" She crossed her arms, an angry frown on her face.

"Because I could win." He pointed from him to her. "We could win the series."

"I don't care about that anymore."

"Of course you do. We both do. We worked hard for it."

"Cruz," she paused and looked away. "A new car will cost more than we'd make on the race."

"That's not the point, is it?"

She unfolded her arms and turned away from him, stalking back and forth. "The point is, I don't have the money to pay you back."

He shrugged. "I know. You gave it all to the hospital. I'm paying for the car."

She looked at him incredulously. "We're both going to be broke. Right back where we started. We . . . it was all for nothing."

He stepped closer to her. "Was it?" They'd found something more valuable than money. They'd found each other. At least, he hoped they had.

"Cruz, keep your money. Go back to school, get your degree, and start your career. I should never have interrupted your education. Your cousin told me how you'd planned out your future, showed me the little flow chart you made and—"

Cruz laughed. "Gabby, screw that flow chart. When you asked me to join you on this venture, I . . . I didn't know what to do. I was so tempted." He touched her chin. "For two reasons: the thrill of racing in a top NASCAR circuit. And being with you."

He placed his hands on her shoulders and pulled her close. "Being an accountant doesn't excite me. Racing excites me. *You* excite me."

A small smile crept up her lips. "So, what do you want now?"

"Hell." He shook his head. "I want the ACRA Menard West Series Cup. Maybe in a few years . . . who knows?"

Her eyes narrowed. "You want to keep racing?"

"Do you?"

He saw the spark in her eyes, then saw it die. "No."

"Why?"

"I can't go through that stress anymore. When I saw all those cars plow into you, when they pulled you out on a stretcher, I, I—" She shook her head. "No, I don't want you to race anymore, Cruz."

He squeezed her shoulders. "And I don't want you to worry about that."

"I don't want to lose you." Gabriela paused, stared at his face, and realized this was it. She'd waited for days to tell him how she felt. She eased out of his grip and looked away, looked at the small house he grew up in, and compared it to the mansion where she'd lived most of her life. How could such a small home hold so much love while her grandiose palace held none?

"I don't want to lose that," she said, pointing to his childhood home, the symbol of what she's always wanted.

He turned and glanced at the house, then frowned. "What? My dad's house?"

"This place is you, Cruz. Warm, full of love and family, full of cherished memories, and hard-working, loyal, real people." She laughed and turned to him. "My God, Cruz, it's what I saw in your eyes when we first met. It's why I fell in love with you back when I was seventeen and had to kiss you."

His eyes widened. "You fell in love with me?"

"It's what Dad saw, too, isn't it? He looked at you, and he saw himself, where he came from, his roots. When he looked at me, everything was new, I was an Americanized kid, and he couldn't relate to me. He had the American dream, but he'd lost this."

"Wait a minute, you said—"

She grabbed his hand. "The letter! He told me in the letter to come to Mexico! He was trying to tell me in his own way, wasn't he? He wanted me to see that the private schools and the big houses and the money were nothing without my roots, without my soul."

"Wait. You're driving me crazy. Did you say—"

"That I loved you. Yes. I do. I love you, Cruz. You're everything I've ever dreamed of. You're passionate, determined, so loyal you make me want to shake you, hardworking, honest, and sexier than any man deserves to be, and—."

He tugged at her arm and closed his lips on hers, giving her a fervent, hungry kiss. She wanted to pull away, finish explaining everything she loved about him, ask him if he was still willing to marry her, but . . . it could wait. She wrapped her arms around him and let herself be dragged into the sensuous flavors of Cruz Ortega.

He abandoned her lips finally and drew a deep breath. "I've wanted to do that for days now."

"You don't have to stop."

"I love you, too." He smiled. "And I want to live the rest of my life with you."

She felt as if her heart would burst. "I want that too." She snuggled deeper into his arms.

"We can have a big wedding and invite everyone we know right after the last race, and—."

"What?" She lifted her head and looked into his eyes. "I thought we agreed no more racing?"

He frowned. "Gabriela, I want to keep racing."

"No."

"No? You're telling me I *can't*."

"Damn it, Cruz. Don't you understand? Now that I have you, when I really know what I want, I can't take a chance on losing it."

He nodded. "I understand, but you taught me something, too. You, *mujer*, have more guts than anyone I know. You taught me to take chances, not give up, and go for it." He kissed the side of her neck. "To risk it all."

She shook her head, she didn't want to risk *him*. "I can't be a part of it anymore. It's over. No more racing."

"I worked hard all season. *I can win*. You have to give me this. One more race, Gabriela. Then if you don't want to do another season, I'll . . . I guess I'll quit. I'll get my accounting degree, find a job, and help you save up for your art school."

She pulled out of his arms. "You're determined to get back in that car?"

"*Yes*, I want this, Gabriela. I can't walk away from it all with my tail between my legs because of one wreck."

She frowned. "Aren't you frightened?"

"Terrified. But I have to do this."

All the joy of a few moments ago vanished, and she felt her fragile newfound future slipping away. "I'm sorry. Do what you have to, but I'm not going to be there to watch you race that car."

CHAPTER TWENTY

November

Sheena picked Gabriela up at LAX and got on the 405 Freeway headed north to connect with the 10 East. Cruz stayed behind with his father for another week. They needed the time together alone.

She gazed out of the window at the ugly traffic, the smog, the graffiti on the buildings. All she wanted was to get back to her apartment and sleep for days.

"Are you listening to me?" Sheena asked. She'd been talking about her parents. They were upset with her. But Gabriela stopped listening to what her mother said, and how she responded, and how the argument ping-ponged back and forth.

Gabriela turned her head and took a long, pensive look at her best friend. She wore her hair clamped up on her head, sporty jeans molded to her long legs, and a red ditsy floral v-neck blouse barely covered her suntanned breasts. She looked young and happy. "Your parents love you," Gabriela said.

"I know, but I'm not ready to be them. I don't want a stuffy house in the Palisades. I don't want a respectable job. I just want to lie around naked with Danny and waste my life away." She laughed. "According to Mom, of course."

Leaning her arm on the door and window and holding her head, she continued to stare at Sheena, who had never experienced real loss, who didn't appreciate the family she had. She envied her. Gabriela understood her need to rebel and not follow the life her parents had planned for her. "How long are you going to do that?"

"What?"

"Spend all day naked and in bed with Danny. When is it over?"

"Gabby?" Sheena shot her a wide-eyed look. "It's just starting. Why are you talking about it being over?"

"You're going to stay with him forever?"

"How should I know?" Frowning as she stared at the traffic up ahead, she turned the steering wheel and merged onto another lane. "Let's stop for dinner. This traffic is ridiculous."

"I'm not hungry. I just want to get home."

"You need to eat. And I do, too." She pulled out in Culver City and found a Ramen place. That sounded kind of good, actually, and maybe she was a little hungry.

After they ordered and waited for their meal, Sheena took Gabriela's hands. "Just be happy for me. One mom is enough."

"I thrilled. I love you both."

Sheena gave her a toothy grin. "I'm writing music. I got an agent and sending lyrics out to artists. The sex is amazing; he's insatiable. What else can I ask for?" She wrinkled her nose. "Okay, a cleaner apartment because he's a pig, but we can work on that."

"So, you're living with him?"

"Yes! Weren't you listening to anything I said?"

Gabriela frowned. "You do know I just came back from a funeral, right? That Cruz nearly died. That we had to spend all our money to buy a new car, so . . . yes, I'm distracted, and exhausted, and . . .." She burst into tears.

"Shit, I'm sorry, Gabby." Sheena put an arm around her shoulders. "I'm so insensitive. How is Cruz?"

"He's fine." Pigheaded. Infuriating. "He and his dad were both okay, really. They were sad about losing their mother and wife, but they seemed happy to be together. I loved being with them."

Sheena leaned her head against the side of Gabriela's. "Maybe I'm not the only one who's lost her heart over a guy."

Gabriela wiped her eyes and nodded. "I absolutely love him, but he's not an easygoing, playful boy. He's intense. He wants so much out of life. Sheena, he's going to race again, and I'm so scared."

"Of course he's going to be in the last race? Did you expect him to stop? That's what you hired him to do."

"But that was before."

"Before what? Before *you* decided he wasn't your driver but your lover. " Sheena drew back and drew in a deep breath. "Please tell me he's your lover."

"Before, I realized that I couldn't survive if something happened to him."

The steaming bowls of noodles arrived, and they drew apart. Gabriela moved the broth, noodles, and vegetables around the bowl.

"Gabby, you would survive. You have to lighten up. Love him. Sleep with him. Enjoy your life as long as you can. You don't have any control over the future, not really. But you do have today."

"You didn't live without a mom, and pretty much without a dad. You don't know what it's like to lose everything. To be afraid to love anyone."

Sheena blinked her eyes and gazed down, her long lashes touching her cheekbones. When their eyes connected again, Sheena nodded. "And yet, you love me. You support all my craziness. You believe in me. You've always gone all in. I could die on you too, Gabby."

"It's not the same. You aren't doing dangerous things."

"Danny took me motorcross riding. Are you kidding me? I saw my life flash before my eyes about four times."

"Oh, well, that's not good. I take that back. Now I'm worried about you, too."

Sheena laughed and dug into her soup. "I'll try to take life a little more seriously, and you a little less, what do you say?"

"I don't know." She sipped some of the broth, and it was savory and creamy and so good. Taking chopsticks, she swirled some noodles and shoved them into her mouth. Nothing would convince her that Cruz continuing to race was a good idea.

"So, you're sleeping together, right?"

"Why are you obsessed with that? Did Danny tell you he caught us kissing?"

"No! When? The sleaze ball. He's in trouble now."

The truth was that Cruz couldn't keep his hands off her. He'd taken her under a huge tree, stretched out a blanket, and made love to her there. They took a very sexy bath together when his father went to the grocery store. Sex wasn't the problem.

Sheena took a sip of water while Gabriela finished off the entire bowl of soup. "You were hungry, see?"

"Starved," Gabriela agreed.

Sheena smiled. "We're going to be okay, the two of us."

Gabriela gazed into the happy depths of Sheena's eyes and nodded. "Thanks for helping me with this team and encouraging me to succeed."

"Hey, what are friends for? Our art school is next."

"We'll see. Let's get back on the road. Now that I'm full, I really need to sleep."

The stands at Irwindale Speedway overflowed with people. The final race of the ARCA Menards West Series. The oxygen in the atmosphere crackled as if electrified, the crowd louder than normal, the excitement tangible. Gabriela's heart thumped so hard she was afraid she'd have a stroke if she didn't calm down.

The race would start in a matter of moments. The drivers sat buckled in their cars, waiting for the green flag to drop. Gabriela sat high in the stands with the fans. Even though she told Cruz she would not come, she couldn't miss the last race, a race he deserved to win. Part of her wanted to be down there with him, but another part was still angry that he was willing to risk his life again. And their future.

Cruz set the pace from the green flag to nearly the end of the race. He often led by an entire straightaway, charging hard. Even though he was not fully healed, he'd come to win, and it showed. If Cruz had any fear or any questions about getting back into a race car, he was not revealing it.

Gabriela sat on the edge of her seat and did not move for the entire first 90 laps, but as he neared the end, the last ten laps, she stood. Everyone stood. Cruz was still leading the pack. He would win.

A crazy feeling of panic wrapped around her heart. She couldn't let him do this alone. When he got out of that car, she wanted him to know she was there, that she'd watched. He'd entered the ARCA Menards West for her, and he would win for them both. When he got out of his car, she had to be there to congratulate him, to tell him how proud she was, how much she loved him.

The final lap would be over in less than a minute. She ran down the stands, taking two and three steps at a time; she ran around the gates and flashed her owner pit pass as she hurried under the tunnel into pit row.

When she got there, her pit crew was ecstatic. Flip saw her and took her hand. Cruz's car was just coming down the home stretch. The screams from the crew were deafening as he crossed the finish line, and the checkered flag pronounced him the winner.

With a smile, Flip kissed her softly on her cheek. "He did it," Flip said in her ear. "Thanks to you, you know?"

She kissed Flip back. 'Together, we all made an unbeatable team."

Cruz pulled in after his victory lap. As he made his exit from the car, he was handed a bottle of Crystal Stream water from a sponsor. He obediently drank half the bottle and then was bathed in champagne. Cameras and reporters all shot a steady stream of pictures and fired questions, which Cruz answered expertly.

She was dying to move closer, to push everyone away and get to Cruz. He turned, called Flip but saw her. "Gabriela," he shouted. The media noticed her then and, like a pack of attack dogs, turned her way.

"How do you feel? Did you know he'd take the series? Were you worried after his last crash? What about next season?"

She stared at Cruz, and he stared back, seemingly shocked to see that she'd come. He'd spent an entire month trying to convince her they needed to finish what they had started. Then they could quit. She'd adamantly told him she wouldn't support him getting in a race car again.

But, last night, when he'd left her apartment disappointed, she'd remembered what his father said about death. She couldn't be afraid to lose Cruz. If they loved each other, death couldn't separate them. She had to allow Cruz to follow this new dream that they'd built together.

One by one, she answered each of the reporters' questions as she pushed toward Cruz.

"And next season?"

She glanced at Cruz again. His Adam's apple bobbled, and he lurched toward her, grabbing her hand and pulling her on top of the car.

"I watched the whole race. You were brilliant," she said, completely out of breath.

"I know you didn't care if we won or not. I know the winnings don't interest you, Gabby. But I wanted to give it to you. I want to give you everything you deserve in life. I love you."

She hooked her arms around the back of his neck and kissed him, with the crew, the fans, and national TV watching.

Finally, she turned to the media. "There will be a few changes next year."

"Yes," Cruz said. "We might leave the ARCA Menards West."

After a large rumble and jumble of whys, Gabriela quieted them. "What he means is, we have a wedding to plan. Then I plan to keep him busy making me a mom."

The pit crew cheered, and Cruz stared wide-eyed. She smiled at him. "Besides, Cruz is a talented driver. He might be ready to enter the NASCAR Xfinity Series next season. We'll see. What do you think, Flip?"

Flip grinned from ear to ear. "A couple more seasons in the Westerns, I think. Let the boy prove himself."

She nodded. "Okay. You heard him. We'll be back for one more season."

She turned and placed a hand on Cruz's face. "Ready for the winner's circle?"

"With you, I'll always be in the Winner's Circle, *mi vida.*"

She smiled and silently thanked her father for leaving her a race car that came with the greatest love of her life.

THE END

Preview of Conquest

If you enjoyed *Built to Win*, you might enjoy taking a trip on cruise with Tess and Logan as they battle over winning the Patagonia account. This office, enemies to lovers romance is not to be missed.

Conquest

CHAPTER ONE

Teresa Romero dropped her purse on her desk and slumped down on her rolling leather chair, which screeched as she leaned back. She took a deep, steadying breath. She was never late for work, but today the gods just weren't on her side.

Not only had she had an ant invasion in her kitchen to contend with when she woke up, and a wet mail to spread out on the living room table because her neighbor refused to fix his sprinkler that hit her mailbox, but on her way to work, the fan belt on her old Toyota Celica finally gave out. She had to walk three blocks in high heels to the Mobile station and persuade the greasy, overworked mechanic to fix her car ahead of the other jobs he had waiting in line. An hour and a half later, she was on her way to Los Angeles again, determined to reach the black and white building which housed the offices of Penguin Apparel Inc.

"Hey Tess," Krystle, a busybody sales rep, paused by her desk. "Heard you got the big Patagonia account."

Teresa frowned. "Where'd you hear that?"

Krystle shrugged. "It's going around." Krystle was physically the blond equivalent of Teresa: large breasts, wide hips, too thin for the large body frame. Qualities that made Teresa self-conscious because of the male attention they attracted. In fact, she tried to minimize the exaggerated shapeliness of her body with respectable business suits. In contrast, Krystal chose clothes that were too tight, too revealing. Teresa admired Krystal for her courage in proudly showing her body, yet she cringed at the spectacle she made of herself.

"Well," Teresa said, placing her purse in the bottom drawer of her desk and straightening in her chair. "No decision's been made, as far as I know."

Her line rang, giving Teresa an excuse to brush Krystle off and get to work. She lifted the receiver to her ear and wiggled her fingers at Krystle; however, she didn't take the hint. She stood in front of Teresa's desk, smiling and listening. From the one-sided conversation, she would, no doubt, decipher what she could and embellish the rest.

Edward Reed's voice eclipsed Teresa's thoughts about Krystle. Mr. Reed wanted to see her in his office right away. *Great, I'm late one day, and the boss notices.* She let him know she was on her way.

"Did he say you got the account?" Krystle asked, eager to spread the gossip. Everyone in the office knew she and Logan Wilde were competing for this account, and she was sure they'd probably even started a pool betting on the one they thought would win.

"No, sorry, Krystle. He didn't say what he wanted."

Teresa left a disillusioned Krystle behind and headed to Edward Reed's office. He welcomed her with a smile. Maybe he wasn't going to lecture her about getting to work on time. Could it be that she actually did get the Patagonia account? Penguin was launching its new wool apparel next season, and all they needed was to set up a reliable supplier for wool. *El Gaucho Estancia* in Argentina was that supplier, and Teresa knew she could handle the buy.

"How are you today, Tess?" he asked absently, barely looking up from a file on his desk.

"Not bad," she lied. Her feet were killing her from walking those three blocks in cute, but uncomfortable Michael Kors pumps. She also noticed a grease smudge on her pale blue skirt that no one else would see. "Is something wrong?"

"No, actually, I think you're going to be pleased with my news."

Though she wasn't asked to, Teresa took a seat, her excitement level going up a few notches. "The Patagonia account?"

"As a matter of fact—"

“Sorry I'm late." Logan Wilde blew in, took a seat beside Teresa, and with the theatrics that typified Logan, gave an exaggerated angelical smile. She was sure *that* was the smile he used to vie for everyone's adoration in the office. He had women jumping to help him take care of his mail, clean his desk, type his reports, and listen to his sob stories about his kids.

"It's all right, it seems you're both running late today," Reed commented.

Logan turned a shocked expression toward Teresa. "*You* were late?"

She ignored the urge to fire back that, unlike his everyday tardiness, this was her first time in three years. She lifted her chin " You were saying, Edward?"

Logan eased his long, wiry body back, overly relaxed, overly confident. "The moment of truth, huh boss?"

"I was just telling Tess that she will be pleased with my decision."

Logan's bright smile dimmed just a touch, and that satisfied her almost as much as what Reed was saying.

"Go on," Logan said.

Edward Reed cleared his throat. "I've thought long and hard about this, and I've found reasons why each of you deserves this account."

Teresa held her breath.

"Tess, you're excellent with people, you put in long hours . . . ." Reed looked at Logan. "And you're a great closer, Logan, a great negotiator."

Teresa and Logan glanced at each other. This was an exciting account, the opportunity to travel to a remote farm at the end of the world. More importantly, it came with a commission that would allow her to pay off her parents' debts and guarantee they didn't lose their family restaurant.

"I've decided," Reed said with a smile. "That I'm going to send you both."

The room was silent. Had she heard right?

"You want to run that by me again?" Logan was actually frowning. She'd never seen a frown on that overly happy, childish face.

"I believe together you can secure the buy and get us the wool account we need. One of you might be able to pull it off, but with you both, we can't lose. Now let's go over the figures——"

"Whoa, wait a minute." Logan stood. "I don't need her tagging along. I can close the deal on my own."

"Well, I certainly don't need you." Teresa's face warmed. *The nerve of that man!*

"No offense, sweetheart, but—"

"My name is Teresa."

"Whatever. He's just letting you go because you're Mexican."

"What?" She bolted out of her seat. "I can't believe you just said that."

"Oh, come on, Tess, I didn't mean that as a racial jab, and you know it. He wants you to translate. I don't need a translator."

"Logan," Reed said harshly. "Sit down, you're being offensive."

"I've never needed help to close an account before."

Neither have I, she felt like screaming back at him, but arguing was senseless. She took her seat.

Reed sighed. "If you must know, Logan, Tess was my first choice. Her language skills are definitely a plus, but besides that, she's a great buyer. I think in this case, though, you're going into macho territory with those sheep shearers, and they're going to want to see male representation. I've thought this through. You're both going."

Logan glared at Teresa. Did he think *she* was pleased with this? Spending the next few weeks with God's gift to women was hardly her idea of fun. Of all the men in her office, she had to get stuck with this arrogant, self-centered jerk. But even worse than that, she'd have to split the commission with him, money she could have given her parents.

He slumped into his chair again. "What am I supposed to be, her bodyguard?"

"You'll have to figure out how you want to approach this. One of you does the talking, the other the paperwork and planning? You decide on the best strategy. The key is to secure the buy at the lowest possible cost. Understand?"

They both nodded.

"Good. When you get there, I want you to tour the Estancia, check out the operation, do quality tests, and if all looks good, arrange the buy."

They both listened silently. Teresa felt she was being handed down a sentence.

"You'll have plenty of time to plan." Edward Reed grinned, and he opened up a file. Leaning forward, he handed a brochure to each of them. "This is the good news. You'll be on a cruise ship which will dock close to the sheep Estancia. It will take you about a week to get there since there are no airports where you're going."

No airports? "But there *is* a small airport in the Santa Cruz province, I read about it when I did my research," Teresa said.

"Well," Reed said. "Technically, you're right, but it's used mostly for cargo. Passenger crafts come in about once a week, and not during the holidays."

"So we're going on a cruise ship?" She asked, unbelieving.

"You sure are," Reed said, the pitch of his voice and enthusiastic gestures indicating he thought he'd just granted her the greatest gift. "Of course, I'm not being too generous. Like I said, since it's the holidays, most transportation won't be running in Argentina. A ship is about the only way to get you there comfortably."

"Can't we drive from Buenos Aires?" Logan asked.

"Believe me, you don't want to drive. Most of the roads in Patagonia, if you can call them that, aren't even paved. No, you'll fly into Buenos Aires and from there, take the ship down the coast."

Teresa's brain was still registering something else he said. "You want us to leave before Christmas?"

"That's right. It's a Christmas/New Year's cruise which will get you to San Julian at the beginning of January. Sheep shearing's done in the summer—their summer."

Teresa's spirit dropped a few more notches. She glanced at Logan, but besides having to share the account with her, he seemed to have no objections. He sat quietly listening, almost brooding.

"I see." Teresa's voice couldn't conceal her disappointment. She'd never missed Christmas with her close family. This would be the first time.

"So, put your other accounts on hold. You leave in a week."

About the author

Lara Rios writes romantic fiction and chick-lit romances that empower women to reach for all their goals, not only the love of their lives, but a life filled with possibilities.

Lara loves to travel, to be out in nature, and to dream up stories that include both. Life is an exciting adventure, and through her books, Lara takes her readers on thrilling, passionate journeys. Lara can be contacted at Lara-Rios.com

Note to Racing Fans

You might notice that some of the race tracks mentioned in this novel are now sadly closed. When I dreamed of writing this story and began plotting the characters and storyline, these tracks were still open. I decided to keep them in, maybe out of nostalgia, or maybe because I wanted to remember them myself.

I hope you don't mind.

Dedication

Years ago, my husband and I spent every weekend at a local speedway, selling raffle tickets to raise money for the Leukemia Society. We were young and childless and wanted to help others. We decided to run a marathon in Alaska in honor of children fighting to survive this disease that kills roughly 480 children per year in the United States.

At the time, I didn't know anything about stock car racing, but by the end of the season, I learned that racing fans were loyal, fun, and generous people.

Build to Win was born way back then, when I wondered what it would be like if two people (one who loved racing, and one who hated it) were forced to work together and take a broken-down car all the way to the finish line.

I dedicate *Built to Win* first to my husband, who has always been by my side, supporting every race I've ever run.

Second, I dedicate the book to those fighting Leukemia or other cancers. Never give up! Stay in the race.

Lastly, to my best friend, Susan, who lost her life to pancreatic cancer last year.

www.ingramcontent.com/pod-product-compliance
Lightning Source LLC
LaVergne TN
LVHW091045080826
845145LV00002B/634

* 9 7 8 1 9 3 1 6 2 7 1 7 7 *